WILL'S WAR

CHERRY COBB

The right of Cherry Cobb to be identified as the
Author of the Work has been asserted by her in accordance
with the Copyright, Designs and Patents Act 1988.

Copyright © Cherry Cobb 2018
Cover © Richard Young 2018

First Print Edition 2018

Edited by Shaun Russell & Will Rees

Published by
Candy Jar Books
136 Newport Road
Cardiff
CF24 1DJ

www.candyjarbooks.co.uk

Printed and bound in the UK by
4edge, 22 Eldon Way, Hockley, Essex, SS5 4AD

I'd like to thank Shaun Russell for picking up Will's War, *and making it great! His knowledge has proved invaluable. I'd like to thank Will Rees (editorial coordinator) for seeing the potential in* Will's War. *Thanks also to Richard Young for the most fantastic cover. It's amazing! And finally I'd like to thank my husband, Tristan, for always believing in me.*

– CONTENTS –

Will   1

Will in Trouble   5

Will Gets a Surprise   13

Will Makes New Friends   24

Will Comes Clean   30

The Search Begins   40

Will Meets Jim   45

A Midnight Adventure   53

Will Survives   58

The Air Raid   65

The Evacuation   73

Life on the Farm   80

The Stash   90

Starting School   95

The Lost Sheep   101

Elizabeth Knows   110

The Escape   118

The Discovery   124

All at Sea   130

Getting Closer   138

Back in London   146

The Reunion   156

– CHAPTER ONE –

Will

Will should have been sleeping. The numbers on his digital clock shimmered softly in the half light: 12:05am. His dog, Rollo, a honey and black, hairy mixture of collie and sheltie, lay sleeping at the foot of his bed, farting nosily, disturbing the still air with the smell of eau de cabbage. The sound of Will's mum's gentle snores filtered into his room. He sighed, then twitched open the curtains beside his bed, exposing the inky starlit sky.

You might wonder what Will was doing awake at this hour when most children are tucked up dreaming of unicorns or becoming a famous footballer or persuading Miss Caudwell, the science teacher, into doing more Bunsen burner tricks with screaming Jelly Babies.

None of these things were on Will's mind. He was thinking about his dad. Earlier that day, in school, his teacher had been discussing families and relationships.

She had talked about family trees and hereditary diseases, and had suggested they all made a questionnaire to give to their family members.

The lesson stirred up feelings Will had buried a long time ago. He didn't have a dad at all. His dad had vanished into thin air before he even knew Will was on the way.

Will flipped his pillow over in search of a cool spot and kicked the duvet off his legs. He had always felt different – incomplete somehow – like he didn't quite fit in. He looked across at Rollo and wondered if puppies minded when they were taken from their mothers. He decided they probably soon forgot with the excitement of being in a new family. Rollo was ten now, and Will couldn't imagine life without him. He was his best friend in the entire world. He didn't make friends easily; being naturally shy he preferred to stay inside imagining and creating magnificent models from Lego.

He turned his head to look at his latest creation. It was a time travelling submarine, and it had taken him ages to build.

First he had sketched the idea on paper and then

spent hours sorting through his Lego to find the right shape or colour brick for each section. As it took shape he recorded his progress on his mobile phone, ready to upload to YouTube. Will liked making short films for other people to watch. It made him feel popular. Perhaps when he was older he would become a famous director. His eyes started to feel heavy. As he drifted off to sleep he imagined himself swaggering about a film set, bellowing orders at actors, while he captured the moment for all time.

'Will, breakfast's ready,' his mum called from the hallway.

Will drifted downstairs, yawning loudly, his mid-length sandy hair flopping over his face, partially covering one eye.

'You're a sleepyhead this morning,' Mum said.

'I was thinking about my Lego model and it kept me awake,' he fibbed.

'You and your Lego, you need to get out more.' She poured orange juice into his glass. 'Why don't you take a ball to the rec. I'm sure somebody will play with you.'

Will sipped his juice. 'I don't even have a ball, Mum!'

He rolled his eyes. 'Anyway it's raining.' Picking up the spoon in his left hand, he sprinkled sugar on his Weetabix.

'OK, OK. I just think you should try and mix more, make a few friends,' she said, sipping her tea.

'I've got Rollo, he's my best friend.'

'What are you going to do with yourself today then?' Mum asked, changing the subject.

'I'm going to finish my model. Then I'm going to teach Rollo some new tricks,' Will said, ruffling Rollo's ears.

'Well, as long as you don't get under my feet. I've got some chores to do, and then I promised Mrs David a cake for her daughter's birthday.'

Will rinsed his bowl before loading it into the dishwasher. 'I won't, Mum. Can you make us a cake too?

Will's mum was famous for her cake-baking skills amongst the other parents.

'If I have time. Run along now,' she said as shooed him out of the kitchen.

– CHAPTER TWO –

Will in Trouble

Will and Rollo thundered up the stairs in their attempt to be first to Will's bedroom. Will opened his curtains fully and sat down at his small, Lego-filled, makeshift desk. 'I'm going to finish this now, boy,' he said to Rollo.

Rollo lay down beside him. Front legs outstretched and resting his head on his paws, he stared unblinkingly at Will.

Will hummed to himself as he clicked Lego bricks together, adding details here and there. 'Maybe I should use wheels as well,' he said. 'Then it could be a land submarine.'

'Woof,' said Rollo.

Will fiddled around trying different sized wheels. *This beats being at school*, he thought. Picking up his phone he turned the camera on, switched it to record and filmed his progress. That done he turned his attention to Rollo.

'Now then, Rollo, I want you to be a champion dog when I film you.' Will wagged his finger at Rollo. Rollo in return gave it a hefty lick and, for good measure, jumped up and licked Will's face.

'Get off, you great lump,' Will said with a laugh. He pushed him off and wiped his face with his sleeve. Looking out of the window, Will noticed that it was still raining.

'We'll go downstairs. There's more room and you can do some tricks,' he said.

Rollo could roll over, shake hands, bark on command and spin, to name just a few of his tricks. Will gave his glasses a wipe and shoved his mobile phone into his pocket.

'Come on then, boy, action.'

Will and Rollo walked into the lounge, a rectangle-shaped room with a TV at one end, a sideboard, and a dining table and chairs at the other. Will pushed the coffee table to one side and stood in the middle of the room.

'Here, Rollo,' he said. 'Sit.' Rollo sat in front of him,

tail thumping the floor. Will pulled his phone from his pocket and switched the camera on.

'Will,' his mum called from the kitchen, 'can you come here a moment?'

Will walked through to the kitchen, camera still running. 'Yes, Mum?'

'Would you like jam or chocolate as your cake filling?' she asked. Will zoomed in on the cake mixture before pointing the phone at his mum.

'Chocolate, please.'

'Do you have to point that thing at me?' she asked, waving a wooden spoon at him.

'Sorry, Mum.' Will turned and walked back into the lounge, still filming.

'Rollo,' Will called. 'Shake hands.' Rollo bounded over, skidding to a halt in front of Will, and proffered his paw.

'Good boy, Rollo.' Will shook his paw and retrieved a dusty dog treat from his jeans pocket. Rollo wagged his large fluffy tail across the carpet, sweeping stray crumbs back and forth.

Will panned his phone around the room, zooming in

on the TV and games console before moving on to the sideboard.

'This is my mum's collection of snow globes,' he said. As he moved the camera around, he paused over the tiny silver-framed photograph of his dad. It was the only one his mum had, and it took pride of place in the middle of the sideboard. The grainy image revealed a thin man with a clean-shaven face wearing a flat cap. He looked happy and relaxed. Will scowled.

Probably pleased he was running away, Will thought darkly.

'Woof, woof,' Rollo barked, fed up of waiting for Will to call him.

'Sorry, Rollo.' Will swung the camera around.

'Roll over, boy,' he said.

Rollo obliged, rolling around on his back, tongue lolling, legs pawing the air.

'Good dog.'

Rollo rolled over and sat up waiting for his next command.

'Spin, Rollo,' he said.

Will stood on the sofa. Rollo span around and around.

'Steady, boy, you'll get dizzy,' Will said, laughing.

Rollo span some more, encouraged by Will's laughter. Without warning his tail knocked the edge of the picture, sweeping it off the side, tossing it through the air and into the wall. The glass smashed as it landed.

'SIT!' Will shouted. He jumped off the sofa and lunged towards Rollo. In mid-air Rollo turned sharply, banging his fat bottom into the sideboard and causing a snow globe to crash to the floor, its snowy contents seeping rapidly into the carpet. Will's mum came running into the room.

'What on earth was that?' she shouted

Will quickly tried to pick up the pieces. 'Sorry, Mum. It was an accident.'

'For goodness sake, Will, you clumsy boy, why can't you just play outside?' She burst into tears.

Shocked, Will shouted back, 'It wasn't me. It was Rollo!'

'And who made Rollo jump? You, that's who. It's time you took responsibility for your actions.' She bent to pick up the broken picture frame.

'It's only a photograph, Mum. You think more of that

than you do of me,' Will said, his voice wavering.

'Now you're being silly, Will,' she snapped back at him, eyes blazing.

Will felt his neck prickle with heat as his face reddened. 'I'm not silly. Grandad doesn't think I'm silly.' He balled his fist. 'I'm going to Grandad's. At least he cares.' Will marched out of the room.

In his bedroom Will flung pyjamas and a change of clothes into a bag. *I wish my dad was here*, he thought.

Slamming his bedroom door shut, he stomped into the bathroom and plucked his toothbrush from its stand. *It isn't my fault*, he thought. He was always getting the blame. It was just like when the washing fell off the line into the mud. His mum had blamed him for that. It wasn't like he was aiming at it with his Nerf gun; he couldn't help it if the bullets didn't fly straight.

He stamped downstairs.

His mum stood in the kitchen doorway. 'I'm sorry I yelled at you, Will.'

Will glowered at her. 'I didn't do it on purpose,' he said.

'You never mean to, Will,' she said with a sigh, 'but

sometimes you don't think before you act.' She turned and walked back into the kitchen.

'Yeah, whatever,' he snapped, shoving his feet into his trainers without untying the laces. He yanked open the front door. 'At least Grandad doesn't think everything's my fault. He doesn't get on my case all the time,' he shouted, before slamming the door with a bang. *That'll show her*, he thought.

Will walked quickly with his head down. He just got *so* angry sometimes. *It isn't like she's perfect!* He yanked a branch off a nearby bush, and breaking into a jog, he rattled it along the park railings. Arriving at Grandad's hot and bothered, he rang the doorbell.

'Can I stay the night, Grandad?' Will asked.

'Yes, of course, son.' Grandad gazed at Will's tear-stained face. 'Does your mum know you're here?' he asked gently.

'Guess so,' Will said with a sniff. 'She probably doesn't care anyway. She thinks everything's my fault.

Grandad steered him towards the kitchen. 'Come and have some lunch. I've just stuck some bacon under the grill. I'll just give her a quick call first.' He picked up the telephone. 'How about I make us blackberry pie for our tea?' he said, patting Will's shoulder. 'I know that's your favourite.'

– CHAPTER THREE –

Will Gets a Surprise

Will tried to catch the drops of sticky black juice with the tip of his tongue. Picking blackberries was thirsty work, but Grandad's pie would be worth it. He had picked quite a few when he noticed a small gap between the bushes. It was a perfect site for a den. It was times like these that Will wished he had a brother to share stuff with.

He put down his bowl of berries and crawled inside to check it out. It was quite a large area covered with tufts of grass and gnarled tree roots. Luckily it hadn't rained for a couple of weeks, so the ground was quite firm. Something was glinting in the sunlight behind a wall of dense bushes. It looked like a tin roof, but it was hard to see through the tangle of branches and brambles. Perhaps it was an old shed.

He inched closer on his belly, his curiosity getting the

better of him. He could just see some corrugated sheets of metal through the leaves. He pushed himself to his feet and hurried over to investigate. His jumper snagged on the thorns as he fought to push the prickly shrubs out of the way.

At last – he was through! In front of him was an old air-raid shelter. He gave a low whistle, his heart thudding in his ears. Grandad had told him about the shelters people built at the bottom of their gardens during the Second World War. It had to be one of those! The door looked like it was made from bits of rough wood nailed together. A waterfall of cream and white ivy clung to it, and green moss crept up the sides in tufts.

Determined to look inside, he shoved it with his feet. It opened slowly. He walked in, rubbing the dust from his hair as his eyes began to adjust to the gloom.

Wow! No one has been in here for years and years, he thought. He could just make out a bench on one side of the shelter, and on the other an old crate standing on its end with a battered saucepan on top. A random summer breeze wafted through the open door and an old newspaper fluttered from the bench to the floor. Will picked it up and peered at it through his thick-rimmed glasses, his hand instinctively reaching for the mobile phone in his pocket. He held it over the paper and let the bright screen illuminate the faded headline. It read: 'Germans Invent Deadly Flying Bomb – the Doodlebug'. Grandad had told him all about the flying bomb; he said they just dropped out of the sky when they ran out of fuel, exploding as they hit the ground. He walked gingerly around, running his fingers along the rusty iron sheets that made up the walls, tucking his nose and mouth into his jumper, and trying not to breathe the stagnant musty smell. He couldn't imagine what it would be like to eat and live in here. Probably awful! He didn't like confined spaces, ever since he had been trapped in a lift when he was five.

Feeling something under his shoe, he bent down and hooked it out of the dirt with his fingernail. It was an old tin soldier, its paint faded and chipped. Instinctively, he pushed it into his pocket and continued to walk further into the shelter. Hidden in the back corner of the wall, at about waist height, was what looked like a small round doorknob. He wrapped his hand around it. It felt cold and smooth in his palm. *Ah, there must be a room at the back where they slept*, he thought. Will jiggled the handle and pushed with his shoulder for good measure.

The door sprang open and he fell through onto hard concrete. Breathing heavily, he wiped his palms on his jeans and gazed at the sky. It was filled with an amber glow. *This can't be right*, he thought.

He stood up and wiped his glasses with the edge of his jumper, hoping that when he put them back on the sky would be a normal colour.

Clouds of thick dark smoke caught at the back of his throat, making him cough. He could hear shouting. Women seemed to be calling for their children. His eyes scanned the street, trying to take it all in, but there were so many people rushing around that all he wanted to do was turn around and run back to the garden.

Before he could move, he felt a hand grab his shoulder, and an elderly man's voice said, 'Quickly, lad, don't loiter in the street. It's far too dangerous. Bombs wait for no one.' Will almost tripped and fell as he was propelled forwards, down some steps into what appeared to be an underground shelter. It was crammed

16

with people, chattering away as if being underground was an everyday occurrence. Snippets of conversation reached his ears. 'Come on over 'ere, love,' a soft, motherly voice said. Will walked over to where the woman was pointing. She tapped the bench beside her.

'Here, take this.' She passed Will a cup of weak tea. 'Warm your insides up. My name's Lily… you okay?' Will tensed. He wasn't supposed to talk to strangers, no matter how friendly they sounded. Something felt very wrong about all this. The air smelled of tea and sweat. His head started to ache as voices clamoured on top of one another, and the ground trembled beneath his feet.

'What's going on?' he said. His voice came out wobbly and uncertain.

'Oh, it's just your usual raid… Hitler trying to get one over us. We'll be out of here before you know it.' Lily's eyes twinkled. 'You must have been in raids before, love, eh?'

Will opened his mouth but nothing came out. Luckily he was saved from answering by the approach of a young boy with dirty knees who began pulling at the woman's dress.

'Mum, Mum, can I have something to eat?' he said.

'Now, where do you think I'm going to conjure up food from?' She patted his head. 'Always thinking of his stomach,' she said to Will, rolling her eyes.

Will blew on his tea, not too sure if he should drink it or not. *A war, she said. How can there be a war on?*

He turned his head and gazed around the room. Everyone had gas masks with them, and they were dressed in drab, old-fashioned clothes. Will picked up a pamphlet that was folded beside him. His hand trembled as he looked at the date: 3rd June, 1943. He clenched his jaw.

This was ridiculous – no, this was beyond ridiculous – it was impossible! How could he have been picking blackberries in the twenty-first century one minute, and then find himself bang smack in the middle of World War Two? He shook his head vigorously and closed his eyes. Maybe it was those berries he'd eaten.

He opened his eyes again. Nothing had changed.

Lily looked concerned as she gently rescued the mug of tea from his trembling hands. A cold shiver ran down his back. *This can't be real.* He shook his head once more.

'Grandad?' he whispered, his eyes frantically searching the shelter. He glanced at the pamphlet again. 'What to do in a gas raid: London'.

Well, I'm in the same city at least, he thought. *Maybe if I just go back outside the door will be there.* 'I have to get out of here. I need to go back,' he said. The words gushed out of him as he leapt to his feet. His legs started to shake uncontrollably.

'You can't go yet, lad, you daft thing.' Lily pulled him back down.

He hadn't realised he'd spoken aloud. He would just have to wait and hope the raid would be over soon so he could escape; he chewed anxiously on his fingernail. 'Shouldn't be long now. You got brothers and sisters then?' Lily asked.

No, just me,' Will said with a sniff. He rubbed his eyes with his knuckles and tried not to cry. Tears were not going to help the situation.

Until a couple of hours ago he had been a normal kid spending the weekend with his grandad, looking forward to going back home to his dog, Rollo, and playing with his Lego.

'Here, mister! Can you play cards with me?'

Will looked up. A small girl, with long straggly blonde hair and blue eyes that seemed far too large for her head, stood beside him. She looked about six or seven. Playing cards was the last thing he wanted to do, but it would take his mind off the fact that he was trapped here – at least until he could figure out what to do next.

'Sure,' Will said, as he let out a gentle sigh.

'I'm Rose,' said the girl, thumping a pack of grubby cards into Will's hand. 'You look a bit like my brother. Your clothes are funny. Were you on your way to a fancy dress party?' She wrinkled her nose as she spoke. Clearly jeans weren't in fashion in 1940s England.

'Err, yes,' Will said, thinking quickly. 'Is your brother here?'

'Mummy says he's an angel in heaven now. Can we play snap?' Will shuffled in his seat, embarrassed, marvelling at how easily Rose seemed to accept the situation. Right now, he wasn't feeling anywhere near as brave. *I'm stuck in an air-raid shelter in World War Two. World War Two! It will be over soon. Yes, over soon.* He repeated the mantra.

He was jerked from his thoughts by the sound of a loud siren.

'All clear! Everybody out!' a man's voice rang out confidently, and immediately people began to shuffle off seats towards the door.

Will hung back, afraid to leave and equally afraid to stay. 'Come on, lad, haven't you got a home to go to?' The warden put his hands on his hips and scowled.

'Sorry,' Will mumbled. He had no choice. He had to move.

He climbed up the steps to the street. The darkness seemed to swallow him up as his heart banged against his chest. Where was the door to Grandad's shelter? He'd completely lost his bearings.

He watched everyone melt into the streets and disappear into houses. A building at the end of the road was on fire – the flames licked the beams and crackled in the heat. Hot air wafted over him in waves and his eyes stung behind his smeared glasses. Fire engines hurtled towards the chaos and debris, their bells clanging. Will's mind went blank. He couldn't think what to do. *I'll have to walk for a bit; maybe I'll recognise something.* He jammed his hands into his pockets, his fingers automatically clasping around his mobile. *Of course, my mobile might have a signal!* He yanked it out and checked the screen – nothing, absolutely no signal, not even one bar. He drew in a long breath and shoved his phone back into his pocket.

'Well, well what have we 'ere then, lads?'

Will looked up to find a gang of youths had surrounded him.

'I think he's a spy, g'vnor,' the tallest lad said, his cigarette glowing as it dangled from his lips. 'He looks shifty enough.'

'Cat got your tongue, boy?' One of the other lads prodded Will in the chest.

'N... No.' He could taste blood as he bit the inside of his cheek to stop his voice from shaking.

'What's that you had in your hand then?' the ringleader said, shoving his face up close to Will, baring a set of rotten yellow teeth, his breath stinking.

Will flinched. 'Nothing.' His hand clutched tightly round his phone. He couldn't let them have that. 'It's just a torch,' he said. 'I'm not a spy.'

The gang moved closer to him. 'I think we should check, boys. Don't you?' They grabbed Will's arms, their fingers pinching his skin through his thin jumper. Will twisted his body and flung his arms over his head to protect himself. The gang tightened around him.

'Search his pockets, lads.'

Will's knees buckled as he slid to the ground. Feeling lightheaded, he held back a scream rising in his throat. He couldn't let them get his phone! He gasped for air. Thoughts of Rollo coming to his rescue flashed through his mind. He prayed for a miracle.

– CHAPTER FOUR –

Will Makes New Friends

'Oi! Get off him.'

Interrupted, the gang fled into the shadows.

Two younger boys approached Will. 'You OK, chum?' One of them touched Will on the shoulder as he crouched down next to him.

'I think so.' Will rubbed his hands up and down his bruised arms. 'Thanks.'

The other boy held out his hand and pulled Will to his feet. 'Don't think you should hang about here, chum. Streets are not safe at night.'

Will thought quickly. 'I was waiting for my mates. We were playing a game and they ran off. I'm not from round here.' Will hoped his lie sounded convincing. It was probably more convincing than the truth: that he was waiting for morning to see if he could find a time rift. His mum always told him one fib would lead to another. She was right… as usual.

'I'm Frank. This is Charlie,' said the slightly taller boy. 'We're twins, although I was born first so I'm the oldest.'

'We're eleven,' Charlie said puffing his chest out. 'What's your name, chum?'

'Will. I'm eleven too.'

'We thought you was a girl at first with that long hair.'

Will raised his hand automatically to smooth his unruly mop. He noticed Charlie's short-clipped hair.

'You're wearing some weird clothes, pal. Never seen anything like that round here.'

Will looked down at his jeans. 'They were a present from a relative abroad,' he said vaguely. After being in the shelter he realised that clothing had been very different in wartime.

'Nice,' said Charlie. 'I can't remember the last time I got a present. Do you want to hang around with us for a while? We're off to the soup kitchen.' He patted his stomach.

Frank nudged Charlie. 'He might not want to come with us.'

'Come on,' said Charlie with a lopsided smile that

matched his hair. 'No point in waiting here.'

Will hesitated and fiddled with his glasses. He didn't really want to go with them, but staying put could be worse; the gang of boys might even come back.

'OK, thanks. But don't you have to get home?' Will thought about his mum and his grandad and how worried they must be. *I bet the police are involved and everything by now.*

'We live with our auntie Doris. Our dad's away fighting, see... and Mum died,' Frank said, dropping his gaze to his scuffed shoes.

'Oh, sorry...' Will thought of his own mum, probably crying right now wondering where he was. He shouldn't have gone off at her like he did.

'S'alright.' Frank shrugged and pushed Charlie forward down the street. Will followed, his spirits lifting slightly.

'Doris is dad's sister,' Frank said, looking over his shoulder at Will. 'Is your dad fighting too?'

Will wasn't sure what his dad did since he had never met him. But he was fairly sure it wasn't fighting. 'Err, I live with my grandad... and my mum,' he said, hoping they would assume that meant his dad was at war. 'Doesn't your auntie mind you being out after dark?' he asked.

'Well, she does, but some evenings she has to work. We are supposed to stay in but—' Charlie grinned and shrugged.

How on earth do they know where they are going, thought Will. It was impossible to see anything in the wartime blackout darkness.

The outline of a church became visible through the shadows. 'This is where we get the soup,' said Charlie. 'It's supposed to be for people who have had their houses bombed, but they don't mind giving us kids some every now and then.'

Will imagined his grandad sitting at home, fretting about his missing grandson. He pictured him sitting in the high-backed chair, crossword puzzle tossed onto the floor, next to the TV guide. 'I'll be back soon,' he mumbled to himself.

The smell of soup triggered a loud rumble from Will's tummy. He hadn't eaten in hours and it smelt delicious.

Charlie passed Will a steaming mug, almost too hot

to hold. 'Thanks, I didn't realise how hungry I was,' Will said, taking a tentative slurp.

Charlie and Frank nodded and carried on drinking theirs. Charlie finished first and wiped his mouth with his sleeve.

'Well, nice meeting you,' Frank said, putting his mug down. 'We'd better head home before our aunt comes back and finds we're not in bed!'

No! They couldn't leave him now! Will felt the sickening panic return as the twins started to walk away. He was totally lost in London – he didn't want to be alone too!

'Wait!' he shouted after them. 'Can I come with you?'

Charlie and Frank looked at one another and raised their eyebrows in surprise.

'You had better go home, pal,' Frank said. 'Your grandad will be worried.'

Will hung his head and shuffled his feet. 'Yeah, suppose,' he mumbled. He hunched his shoulders and headed towards the door.

'See ya,' he said over his shoulder. The hot soup had warmed his stomach, but the night felt cold and unfriendly as Will pushed open the church door and stepped outside. The clouds had fled and the temperature was dropping. He shivered in his thin cotton jumper. *Wish I had a jacket*, he thought.

Charlie felt uncomfortable. 'Perhaps we should have let him?' he said to his brother. 'He looks like he could do with a friend right now. Maybe he lied about his grandad? He might not have any family.'

Frank wasn't so sure. 'He must have, he doesn't look like an orphan.'

'*Come on*… Auntie won't mind,' Charlie pleaded.

'Oh, OK, but you can ask her,' Frank said. He always gave in to his little brother – even if he was only younger by five minutes.

'Come back, Will!' yelled Charlie. 'You can join us if you like.'

Will turned and smiled. 'Really?' he said, running back.

'Yeah, come on.' Frank put his arm around Will's shoulders. 'You'll have to bunk up with us though.'

Will glowed. It was weird but he felt like he had known Charlie and Frank for a long time.

– CHAPTER FIVE –

Will Comes Clean

'**A**nd just where do you think you've been?' Auntie Doris looked up from her knitting and frowned, the deep lines in her forehead sinking further into her round face.

Charlie nudged Frank. 'Sorry. We heard a noise outside and we was worried. We went to check and that's when we found Will here. Can we put him up for a bit?'

'Haven't you got a home to go to, Will?' she asked, looking over the top of her needles, which continued to click crossly.

Will swallowed. 'Um, my parents are away and I was staying with my sister, but she's had to go to the hospital.' He paused. 'It was an emergency. I said I could stay with friends, but then I got lost.' He chewed his lip and hoped it sounded believable.

'Well, as you're here now...' Auntie Doris stuffed her

needles into a fat ball of green wool and gave him a tight-lipped smile.

'Thank you,' said Will with a nod.

'Come on, let's show you your billet,' Charlie said.

The twins shared a small box room at the back of the house. There were only two bedrooms and, to Will's horror, no loo.

'Don't you have a toilet?'

'Yeah, course.' Frank looked puzzled. 'At the end of the garden... in the outhouse, isn't yours the same?'

Will was finding it increasingly tricky to dodge these questions. 'My sister has one in the house, out the back of the kitchen.' He said, trying to remember a recent school trip to a war museum.

'Lucky you!' Charlie nudged him. 'Ours is freezing in the winter.'

Will glanced about the room. It was nothing like his back home. Two beds stood side by side; a small bedside cabinet with a lamp was wedged in between. The beds, he noticed, had blankets tucked tightly around the mattresses. There were no duvets.

'We'll bunk up together tonight, Will, so you can have

a bed to yourself,' Frank said.

'Thanks, but I don't mind sharing,' Will said, desperate to please his new friends.

Frank laughed. 'What… and have to put up with Charlie's stinky feet?'

'Oi, me feet don't stink!' Charlie went to swipe Frank, but he ducked out of the way.

'Your socks do.' Frank held his nose and pretended to faint.

Just then, Auntie Doris yelled from the bottom of the stairs. 'You'd better be in bed by the time I come upstairs,' she said.

'We was wonderin' why you didn't find your friends?' said Frank and Charlie in unison, as they started to get undressed. They laughed – they were always doing things like that – saying the same thing at the same time.

Will thought how to reply. 'The thing is,' he said after a few moments of silence. 'I didn't quite tell you the truth.'

'Knew it,' Frank said.

'I made the bit about friends up,' Will said quickly. 'But I do have parents. They're just not here.' He waved his arm expansively.

'Fallen out with them, is that it?' asked Frank.

'No, nothing like that.'

'Have they died?' Charlie asked dramatically.

Will hesitated. *They haven't been born yet*, he thought.

'You'd better tell us, pal, or we'll have you back out on the street.' Frank frowned at Will. 'Can't be too careful in wartime, you could be a spy for all we know,' he said pushing his face into Will's.

Will longed to tell them; they might even be able to help him. But would they believe him? He scarcely believed it himself. His gut feeling told him he could trust them, but there was still a nagging doubt that people might think he was crazy and call the police. He could get locked up! After all, this was 1943... why *would* anyone believe him?

'If I tell you, you must promise not to say a word to anyone.' Will bit his lip and held his breath.

'We promise,' they said solemnly, their eyes wide.

Will rubbed his hands nervously. 'The thing is,' he started, 'I wasn't born in this time... I was born years from now in the future.'

'You fibber!' Charlie said. 'You're trying to dupe us.'

'I'm not,' Will said hotly. 'I'm telling you the truth.'

'Cor,' Charlie said, raising his eyebrows. 'Come to think about it. I did think there was sommat a bit different about you. Didn't you, Frank?'

'Yeah,' agreed Frank, drawing out the word in a long drawl as he studied Will.

'You don't sound nothin' like us, and your clothes, well…'

Will examined the twins in the dim light of the bedroom. He could just about tell them apart. Frank was slightly taller and thinner than Charlie; they both had blue eyes and short-cropped brown hair, although Charlie had a bit of a quiff at the front that curled on the edge of his forehead.

'So, how did you get here then?' asked Charlie, who had sprawled out on the bed next to his brother.

Will sat down on the other bed and took a deep breath. 'I think… I fell through a time rift.'

'A what?' asked Charlie. 'Never heard of one of those.'

'One minute I was in my grandad's old shelter… the next I was here in 1943, in the middle of World War Two.'

'What are you going to do now?' Frank asked.

'I've got to try and get home. I can't stay here. What if people find out? They might think I'm mad or something. Anyway...' He sniffed. 'I miss my grandad and my mum – and Rollo of course. They'll be so worried about me. I thought that tomorrow I would go back to that air-raid shelter. Maybe I'll find a door there somewhere. Can you take me back to the place where you found me? I haven't a clue how to find it again.'

'We could try, but you need different clothes. Do you want to borrow a pair of my trousers?' Frank said, practical as ever. He leapt off the bed and dragged out a pair from the chest of drawers. 'These are my only other pair – for best, see? Try them on.' He passed them to Will, who was a bit taller than Frank. Will slipped off his jeans carefully – he didn't want his mobile to fall out of the pocket – and tugged on the trousers. They were made of grey flannel and were bit short. They itched terribly too. He was glad his friends couldn't see him dressed like this; he would never hear the end of it.

'Better not tell Auntie,' Charlie said to Frank. 'She'll kill you!'

Will started to take them off.

'It's OK, pal, you borrow them, I don't mind.' Frank slammed the drawer shut and returned to sit on the bed.

'Thanks,' Will said, buttoning them back up. He was folding his jeans when he remembered the tin soldier buried in the pocket. He pulled it out and slipped it into his new grey trousers. *It might bring me luck*, he thought.

Charlie grinned and flicked his hair out of his eyes with his fingers. 'What's it like? The future?'

'Well...' Will said. 'Nearly everyone has a flat-screen TV... and a games console... and a mobile phone.'

'A mobile phone?' Charlie asked, scratching his head. 'Eh?'

'It's a telephone that fits into your pocket.'

'Nah, now you're just making it up!' Frank punched him on the arm, chuckling. 'Good joke though, I nearly fell for it!'

'Everyone knows a telephone can't fit in a pocket silly,' Charlie said. 'They need a box and wires and everything.'

'Look,' Will said. 'I'll show you.' He pulled his mobile phone from his jeans pocket and clicked on a couple of photos. 'These are photos I've taken with the camera on my phone.'

The boys stared, speechless.

'You can make films with it as well,' Will said.

'Films?' Charlie said. 'Like you get at the pictures?'

'Sort of,' Will said. 'But shorter. Look I'll show you.' He clicked on the video he had taken of Rollo. 'That's my dog,' he said. 'I filmed it in the lounge. Look, you can zoom in on stuff too.' He zoomed in on Rollo.

'Can I have a go, Will?' Charlie said, his eyes sparkling.

'Yeah, only quickly though, or my battery will go flat.'

'What do you mean flat?' asked Frank.

'If I don't charge it the battery will run out,' explained Will.

Frank hung over Charlie's shoulder as he zoomed in and out of the film clip, his mouth wide open. 'Wait,' he said. 'Who is that chap in the photograph?'

'My dad,' replied Will curtly, putting his hand out to take the phone from Charlie.

'Cor, he looks a bit like Jim.'

'Nothin like him.' Charlie dismissed Frank's idea. 'He hasn't got a beard for starters.'

'People grow beards, dummy.' Charlie goaded Frank.

Will turned the phone off and slipped it back into his pocket. 'Who's Jim?'

'Jim is our pretend uncle.'

'Pretend?' Will frowned. 'I don't understand.'

Charlie laughed. 'Not pretend as in made up, pretend as in uncle.'

Frank came to his rescue. 'He is an old friend of our auntie's. We sometimes call him Uncle Jim.'

'Oh right, I always call my mum's best friend auntie too,' Will said.

'It must be amazing to just be able to look at stuff when ever you want to, that's out of this world,' Frank said, excitedly. 'And it's a telephone as well. Blimey.'

'Yep, cool, isn't it?' Will grinned. He was relieved they hadn't asked him what the Internet was.

'It must be fantastic living in the future,' Charlie said. 'Could we come back with you?'

'No!' Will said, taking his clothes off and laying them at the bottom of the bed. 'It wouldn't be right.' He got into bed as the boys looked at each other slightly miffed.

'Do you think he's tellin' the truth, Frank?' whispered

Charlie, after they heard gentle snores coming from Will.

'I dunno.' Frank furrowed his brow. 'How do we know people can't time travel? Remember that book we had to read in school, *The Time Machine*? Some bloke invented a machine that went through time, didn't he?'

'Yeah, but Will didn't come in a machine, did he?' Charlie said.

'No, I suppose, but then how did he get that phone?'

Charlie thought for a bit. 'I don't know, but I wish we had stuff like that.'

'I reckon he's tellin' the truth,' Frank said. 'We'd best keep a close eye on him though, just in case.'

'Good idea,' Charlie said with a yawn. 'Budge up a bit.' He rolled onto his side and pulled the blanket up over his shoulder.

Frank stared into the darkness. He hoped Will was telling the truth; they were in a whole lot of trouble if he wasn't.

– CHAPTER SIX –

The Search Begins

Auntie Doris had made them all some porridge for breakfast. Will was still quite hungry and wolfed it down in minutes.

'Don't you guys have a toaster?' Will asked, looking around the sparse kitchen. 'Or a freezer for that matter,' he added.

Frank hesitated, spoon halfway to his mouth. 'Toaster?' he said sounding puzzled.

'For making toast,' Will explained.

'Goes under the grill, chum. You'll be saying do we 'ave servants next. Toaster indeed!'

'Everyone has one where I come from,' Will said.

'I've heard of them. Our cousin Ruby is in service and she uses one,' Charlie said. 'Not heard of a freezer though.'

'A freezer is where you keep stuff cold, like ice cream and chips. It's a bit like a freezing-cold cupboard.'

Charlie snorted. 'A freezing-cold cupboard, now that would be funny. Imagine putting your pullover in there... or your pants!' He sniggered.

Will sighed. Some things were proving very hard to explain.

'Come on,' Frank said, finishing his porridge. He led Charlie and Will upstairs.

'Here, you'll need this,' Charlie said as he passed Will a gas mask.

'How do I put it on?' Will said.

'You really aren't from round here,' Frank said, grinning.

Charlie gave Will a demonstration, but it took Will a bit of practice before he mastered it.

'We're off, Auntie,' shouted the twins as they headed for the door.

'Make sure you look for your sister today, Will,' Auntie Doris said.

'We're going to help him, Auntie,' chorused Frank and Charlie.

'Just stay out of trouble.'

*

London looked very different in the daylight. The streets were littered with bits of wood, rubble and glass. Everything was covered in a thick layer of dust – you could almost taste it. Some of the houses had their windows blown out, and he could see the walls were covered in black soot. Many others were just ruins. Rose-patterned wallpaper flaked off walls, and a fireplace hung precariously from the shattered remains of a bedroom. Women and children sifted through the remains of homes and lives, looking for lost belongings. Emergency vehicles were still working hard to put out fires and round up injured people.

Will had never seen such devastation. It looked like an earthquake had struck right in the middle of the street. Fragments of fallen bricks and bits of wood lay blasted over the pavement, tripping him up. His mouth hung open, slack with shock.

'This is terrible,' he said. 'How do people live like this?'

'Whatcha mean?' Charlie said. 'It's always like this.'

'Just look around.' Will lifted his shoulders and waved his arms around. 'This looks nothing like London to me.'

'Why?' Frank scratched his head.

Will rolled his eyes and tried to explain. 'All these people—' His voice trailed off as he watched two men carrying a child out of a building on a stretcher.

'We's used to it,' Charlie said with a shrug. He looked across the road. 'Auntie keeps saying it can't last much longer, she says we just have to keep our spirits up. That's all anyone can do.'

Will knew exactly how long the war would last and decided that it was best he did not mention it.

'Come on, Will,' Frank said, 'it'll be quicker if we split up to take a look around.'

'But what are we looking for exactly?' Charlie said.

Will scratched his head. 'I'm not sure really. Maybe a building with a door that looks out of place – or an alley that's just a dead end. He realised how feeble it sounded; they really were looking for the proverbial needle in a haystack.

'Righty-o. See you back here in half an hour then,' Frank said and strode off.

Will walked up and down the road, peering down

side streets, desperate to find something – *anything* – that looked familiar. The porridge lay heavy in his stomach, which was twisted with knots of worry. He could feel sweat on the back of his neck. Nothing looked... well, *right*. Will's eyes darted back and forth. Drawing in a long breath, he turned back to meet Frank and Charlie.

'Anything?' he said, when they had reunited.

'Nope, not a sausage,' Charlie said. 'Which is a pity really, as I'd kill for a sausage!'

Frank nudged him. 'Sshh, Charlie, you're always bein' the clown.'

'How can you joke?' Will snapped at Charlie.

'Sorry...' Charlie said sheepishly.

'Come on, Will.' Frank nudged him. 'Let's head back.'

'We can't just give up!' Will stamped his foot. 'This is *my home* we're trying to find... which we *have* to find,' he corrected himself. 'I can't stay in 1943 forever!'

– CHAPTER SEVEN –

Will Meets Jim

Suddenly Charlie piped up. 'Hey, why don't we take Will to see Jim? He was always telling us about his crackpot adventures. He used to talk about travelling in time, didn't he?'

'He just made that up, stupid,' Frank said, rolling his eyes.

'But what if he didn't? What if it was true?'

'Course it's not true.'

'Can I meet him? Can I? Maybe he can help me?' Will's voice rose in a mix of excitement and desperation.

'OK,' Frank said with a sigh. 'We can see if he's home, but don't get your hopes up, Will.'

I could be home by teatime tomorrow, thought Will. 'Come on.'

'This way then.' Frank turned and led them under a nearby railway bridge.

Will's pace slowed the further they walked. He dawdled past the still smouldering scenes of horror, shocked and bewildered by what he saw. It was all so different from the future… at least where he lived, anyway.

'Don't you have to go to school?' Will asked the boys.

'Sometimes,' Charlie said. 'But it's been bombed out, so we take it in turns.'

'Take it in turns?' Will asked.

'Yeah, like the little ones go in the mornings and we older kids go in the afternoons.'

'Wow, lucky you! We have to go every day until three o'clock,' Will said. 'What do you do when you're not there?'

'Sometimes we invent games, or kick a ball around or play tag,' Frank said.

Will nodded slowly.

'One of the best things to do is collect shrapnel,' Frank continued. 'I've got loads. You can have a look at my collection later.'

'What do you do with it?' asked Will.

'Swaps really. Some're better than others. I got part

of a nose cone the other day! Flippin' 'eck, did everyone want to swap with me then.'

Will tried to look interested, but secretly he thought it sounded very dull and not that much fun.

'Course, we go to church on Sundays. That takes up half the day,' Charlie said. 'Do you go to church, Will?'

'Err, no, not really.'

The boys looked shocked

'But sometimes I go at Christmas with Grandad to the carol service,' he quickly added.

'Mind out lad! Watch where you're going!'

The brusque tones of a woman brought Will out of his thoughts. He had nearly tripped over a small boy clutching his mother's hand as they waited in a very long queue for the butcher's shop.

'S… s… sorry,' Will said with a stammer.

'Why is there such a long queue?' he asked the twins.

'Rationing, ain't it,' replied Frank. 'Gotta queue for everything.'

'Yeah, and then you still don't get it,' grumbled Charlie. 'I can't remember the last time I had jam.'

'Or chocolate,' Frank said, licking his lips.

Will shuddered. *Thank goodness I don't live here,* he thought. So far he hadn't seen anything that even remotely compared to his life back home.

After about quarter of a mile they came to a little side street.

'Here we are,' Frank said. 'Jim's house is about halfway down.'

Will looked at the row of terraced houses. They seemed very small and drab; the walls were painted black with soot. Strips of tape were strapped across the windows like grubby bandages, protecting the glass from bombs.

'It's only us, Jim!' shouted Frank as he opened the door. 'We've brought a friend to meet you.'

They walked through the hallway towards the kitchen, or scullery, as Frank called it.

'Well, well, well… what do we have here?' boomed a cheerful voice. Jim appeared in the kitchen doorway with a tatty tea-towel slung over his shoulder and a mug of tea in his hand. He was a thin, wiry man, with a white bushy beard, highlighted with wisps of grey. Jim was very proud of his beard, despite the fact that it often housed a few stray crumbs of toast. 'You're just in time – must have heard the kettle whistle! Sit yourselves down there and I'll make another pot. Then you can introduce me to your, err… friend.' His voice grew very quiet, and he studied Will carefully for a few moments before turning to place the kettle on the stove.

Will sat down on the edge of the nearest chair and listened to the chink of cups and the slop of milk into a jug. The room was sparse, containing only a range, a sink and a couple of cupboards. There were none of the gadgets that Will was used to seeing in his kitchen.

'Now then, what have you boys been up to? Trouble, no doubt,' Jim said. He was smiling, but he was looking at Will, not the twins.

Frank and Charlie grinned back. 'What us, never!'

'And what's your name?' he said to Will, looking directly into his eyes.

'Will, sir,' Will said.

'We found him, and he needs your help,' Charlie said. 'He's the same age as us.'

They all turned to look at Will.

Will cleared his throat and said, 'Err, I'm not sure how

to explain this really, but I seem to have come here from the future… by accident.'

Jim pressed his fingers together and rested them under his chin. 'Go on then, lad, explain it all to me.'

Will glanced at the twins. They nodded their heads.

'Come on, spit it out, your secret's safe with me.' Jim poured Will a cup of tea and sat back in his chair, one leg crossed over the other.

Here goes nothing, Will thought. He began to tell Jim how he had fallen through an old air-raid shelter in the future and found himself in 1943.

Jim listened carefully. Not even Charlie made a sound.

'So that's it,' Will said. 'Only Charlie told me you know a bit about time travel, sir. Is that true?'

Jim stared at Will for a long time before answering. Finally he said, 'Yes, lad, it is true. I have experienced time travel.'

Charlie and Frank gasped.

'Told you,' Charlie said, digging Frank in the ribs.

'Do you know how I could get back?' asked Will, allowing himself to feel hopeful at last.

Jim had a faraway look in his eye. 'It was a very long time ago, son, and it was different for me. I would advise you to go back to exactly where you arrived here, and see if you can find the time rift that would take you back.'

'But that's just it!' exclaimed Will. 'I don't know exactly where I arrived. It was so dark and I was in shock. I was pushed down into a shelter before I had a chance to realise what had happened.'

'Why was it different for you, Jim?' Frank said.

But Jim would say no more about it.

'Please, sir,' Will said. '*Please* help me.' A trickle of tears fought their way out and this time Will didn't stop them. The knots in his stomach multiplied.

Jim took his time clearing up the cups, teapot and milk. Will watched his every move, afraid to utter another word. Finally, Jim eased himself down at the table again and asked, 'Where did you come through, lad?'

'Frank thinks it was King George Road.'

He nodded. 'That makes sense.'

'Why?' Charlie said.

'I think there is a time rift there.' Jim stroked his

beard, dislodging a stray biscuit crumb. 'I will try and help you, but it could be dangerous, understand?'

Will nodded.

'Meet me at King George Road tonight. I have a plan, but it might not work.'

'I don't care,' Will said. 'I *have* to try.'

'Cor, exciting innit?' Charlie said to Frank.

'Sure is! Devilishly exciting knowing two people who have time travelled.' Frank drummed his fingers on the table.

'You mustn't tell a soul. That's very important. We don't want the coppers on us.' Jim frowned at them. 'You promise?'

'We promise!' they all chorused.

– CHAPTER EIGHT –

A Midnight Adventure

Jim stood at the window watching the boys walk down the road. He hoped he could help Will return home.

He thought back to the day he found his way to the future. He was working in a small greengrocer's shop at the time and had gone down to the cellar to get a sack of potatoes.

He opened the door to what he believed was a cupboard and walked out the other side into... well... the future. Of course it was bewildering at first, but once he found that he could travel freely through the door, he made frequent visits. He made friends and even started courting a young lady. Her name was Susan.

They started to spend a lot of time together, and she wanted to settle down and get married. But whilst Jim enjoyed going back and forth, he realised he couldn't make his life with her. It would be too difficult. Their worlds were so different.

So one day he had decided to leave. A decision he'd always regretted. By the time he had changed his mind, the greengrocers had changed hands and become a pawnshop. He went in afterwards to see if he could get to the cellar, but the owner had put a counter right across the length of the shop. There was no chance of him returning to the future. But if they could break through, there would be a chance. For Will at least.

'Sssh,' Frank said. He flapped his hand at Charlie and Will as they crept down the stairs. 'Mind the last step,' he whispered. 'It creaks in the middle.'

Charlie hopped up and down as Frank gently closed the scullery door. It's been ages since anything exciting happened around here. Come on!'

'We need to watch out for the ARP Wardens,' Frank said.

'Who?' Will said.

'The ARP,' Charlie said. 'The Air Raid Precautions Wardens. They patrol the area keeping a lookout for aeroplanes and stuff, but if they see us we might get into trouble. You just gotta keep your head low.'

The boys walked to King George Road, ducking into the shadows whenever they saw the wardens.

Jim was waiting for them on the corner.

'You made it then?'

'Course,' grinned Charlie. 'We're good at being stealthy.'

Jim looked him in the eye. 'Yes, lad, that's what worries me sometimes. These streets are not a playground. 'Follow me then.'

Jim led them round the corner to the back of the pawn shop. There was a wire fence surrounding the back yard.

'Right, I'm going to cut a hole in the fence so we can get through. You boys keep your eyes and ears open.' He produced a pair of wire cutters from his bag and began to snip away at the bottom of the fence.

'You first,' he said to Frank.

Frank got on all fours and crawled carefully through the jagged hole. 'I'm in,' he hissed. Jim looked relieved.

'Me next,' Charlie said, bending down and wriggling through.

Jim quickly checked behind him as they followed the twins.

Will's heart leapt with excitement.

Jim shone his torch briefly at the storeroom, checking the lock.

'Thank goodness,' he breathed. 'The door's only got a small padlock and chain on it. We'll be inside in no time.'

Will turned and gave Charlie and Frank a brief hug. 'Thank you so much for helping me.'

'It's been great fun, hasn't it, Frank?' Charlie said.

'Yeah, remember us when you get to the future.' Frank bent to tie his shoelace.

'Done it!' Jim grinned as the door to the storeroom swung open.

They peered into the blackness. 'What now?' Will asked.

'We'll go in and look around. I'm guessing there will be a doorway hidden in the back somewhere.' Nobody touch anything.' Jim raised his voice slightly. 'It could be very dangerous.'

The boys followed Jim into the building. There were

shelves stacked with old clothes, ornaments and bags that people had pawned.

'There!' Jim shone his torch at the back corner where the shelves ended. 'I reckon it's there, Will.'

As he turned to show Will, the ground beneath their feet began to shake. 'A raid! Quick everyone out now!' shouted Jim above the rumble of planes.

Jim and the twins ran for the doorway and out through the fence, just as the building next to them collapsed.

– CHAPTER NINE–

Will Survives

As Will clutched his throbbing head he could feel a lump forming. *What had happened?* His brain felt foggy as he struggled to remember. *The Shelter. That was it. He was about to go through the time hole.* He tried to sit up and realised his foot was trapped.

'Help!' he yelled over and over, his voice echoing around him. He tried to brush his hair out of his eyes but his forehead felt sticky. *I'm bleeding,* he thought.

And then he passed out.

'Where's Will?' Frank shouted as he dragged himself up from out of the rubble. 'We need to go back and see if he's is OK.'

Jim's face was black; his eyes were now the focal point of his face. 'I'll try, but you two must wait here. Understand?'

The boys nodded. 'OK,' they said meekly.

Jim trudged into the shadows, his shoulders slumped. He should have never brought Will to this place. He approached the door and shone his torch. It had been blasted off its hinges. Gingerly he went inside, stepping over some broken shelves. He could just make out Will amongst the debris.

'Will!' he shouted. 'Are you OK?'

Will groaned. 'Help,' he said weakly.

'Don't worry, lad. I'm here now.' Jim inched closer to Will, shining his torch up along his crumpled body.

'You've cut your head, son. Try to drink some of this.' He poured some tea from his flask and placed his arm under Will's neck to prop him up. 'I think your leg is trapped,' he added.

'What happened?'

'A bomb, son. We are all lucky to be alive.'

'Where are Charlie and Frank? Are they OK?'

'Don't you worry about them, they're fine. We need to get you out of here.' He tried to move the shelf that lay over Will's foot.

'Ouch,' Will yelped.

'Sorry, son.' Jim wiped his forehead with his hanky.

'I'm going to tell the twins to go for help. The first-aiders will be out and about. Lie still. I'll be back as soon as I can.'

'Don't go.' Will grabbed Jim's jacket. 'I'm… I'm afraid of spiders.'

'There won't be any spiders here, lad, they will have all run off when the building collapsed. Here, I'll leave you the torch. Just don't keep it on or the battery will run flat, OK?'

'OK. Please hurry,' Will said as he clutched the torch to his chest. He had been afraid of spiders ever since a camping holiday with his mum when he had woken up with one crawling across his face.

Charlie leapt up. 'I can see Jim!'

'Quickly, boys, I need you to get help. Will's hurt his foot and he's trapped.'

'I'll go,' shouted Frank as raced off to get help.

'I'll sit with Will,' Jim said. 'You'd better wait by the fence for Frank.'

'Will he be alright?' asked Charlie.

'I hope so, son. I hope so.'

Will had just begun to drift off again when he suddenly felt someone beside him. 'Only me, son, help is on its way,' Jim said, wriggling to make himself more comfortable. 'Tell me about home,' he said, hoping that would take Will's mind off his foot.

'Well,' Will said, 'I come from the future, as you know. We live in London. My mum is called Susan, she works part-time in a shop.'

'That's nice. I knew a Susan once,' Jim said, sighing.

'Sometimes my grandad looks after me when she's working, and I have a dog called Rollo. He's my best friend.'

'I've always lived in London too,' Jim said. 'Though it's not so nice now.' He wiped some bomb debris from his jacket. 'Do you have brothers or sisters?'

'No, it's just me and mum.' Will sipped at the tea. 'Were you married?' He asked Jim.

'Me. No, lad. Came close though.' Jim heaved a heavy sigh. 'What about your dad, Will?'

'I don't have a dad.' Will flicked some rubble with his fingers. Mum said he left before I was born. Just disappeared into thin air. Nobody could find him. I don't think he knows about me.'

Jim had become very still. 'Do you know your dad's name?'

'What?' Will was gazing into the distance, thinking about grandad. *He might be just the other side of this wall,* he thought.

'Your dad's name?' Jim prompted.

'James, I think. Can I have some more tea, please?' Will felt better for talking about his family, stronger somehow.

Jim passed Will the tea. *It couldn't be,* he thought. *It would be too much of a coincidence surely.* He studied Will's face, and yet…

'I think I'm your dad,' he blurted out before he could stop himself.

Will spat his mouthful of tea out. 'My dad! But how?'

'I might be wrong, but I think my Susan is your mum. I really did travel through time, you know. I was meant to meet her but I couldn't get back through the time rift. She said she wanted to tell me something.'

'But she said my dad was called James?'

'Jim is short for James.' Jim took Will's hand. 'I have never met anyone who has time travelled until now. That can't be just a coincidence.'

Will snatched his hand away. He didn't know whether to laugh or cry. For years he had hated his dad for leaving him and his mum, and now Jim was saying that he was his father. It was too confusing. He needed time to think.

'Hello, what have we here then?' The roundish face of a policeman appeared from the gloom.

'This boy has trapped his foot.' Jim indicated the bar lying across Will's leg.

'Don't worry, we'll soon have him out. All in a day's work.'

Will stumbled out of the rubble, his foot bandaged and a sticking plaster on his head. He limped to where the twins were waiting.

'Thank God you're safe,' they said in unison.

'Best you get off home now, kids.' Jim punctuated each word like he was being stabbed. 'I'll see you soon.'

Will looked at him. 'I have to get home. Can we try

again?'

'Sorry, son you will have to wait a few days,' Jim said as he tugged at his beard. 'I've got to go away, we'll have another go when I get back.'

Will's face dropped. 'But…'

'No buts.' Jim held up his hand. 'A few days won't make much difference. Now run along, all of you.'

The boys slunk into bed just before dawn. Exhausted they spent the next day just hanging around the house. Will's foot throbbed and his head still ached a bit. They had to tell Auntie that he had tripped over in the dark on the way to the toilet. Will was quiet and thoughtful. *Can Jim really be my dad*, he wondered.

'I want to try again tomorrow,' he said as they lay about on their beds.

'Bit risky, chum after yesterday,' Frank said as he furrowed his brow.

'It might be may last chance. You saw the building.' Will put his hand to his throbbing head. 'Please guys.'

'Course we will,' Charlie said, leaping up to pat Will's back. 'We're pals, ain't we?'

– CHAPTER TEN–

The Air Raid

'**E**verybody up!' shouted Auntie Doris.

Will opened his eyes blearily. Auntie Doris was standing in their bedroom with a candle in one hand, pulling the blanket off him with the other.

'Get out of bed. Hurry now.' Her tone was urgent, with just a touch of hysteria.

Will could hear the wail and howl of an air-raid siren, and the drone of planes fast approaching.

'Quickly!' Auntie said, pushing the boys down the garden to the Anderson shelter. 'They're getting closer.'

Just as they threw themselves into the shelter, they heard the massive *crump crump* of bombs falling nearby.

'Saints alive!' cried Auntie. 'That was close.'

The planes flew overhead, low and fast. The noise was deafening – chilling! Will had never heard anything like it, not even on the telly. He covered his ears. The whine of the German planes made his knees tremble. He could feel the ground as it moved beneath his feet. He looked over at the twins. They appeared to be dozing on the makeshift bunk, clearly used to the drama of frequent raids. *We're going to die! I'm going to die!* He pressed his hands harder against his ears and squeezed his eyes shut.

After what seemed like hours, the 'all-clear' signalled that the raid was over. They trooped out of the shelter and looked in horror at the sight before them. Their house stared back; the windows had been ripped out and the scullery door was swinging on one hinge. The house next door was even worse. It looked like a knife had sliced right through it. The upstairs floor jutted out; a bed and a wardrobe stood in the middle of the room, the curtains flapping in the breeze. It looked like a doll's house.

'That settles it!' Auntie said, through her tears. 'Frank, Charlie, I'm sending you to stay in the country. I've had the billeting officer banging on the door on more than one occasion telling me London is far too dangerous for children.'

'But—' Frank said.

'No buts! I'm putting you on the train first thing. Will,

I'm sorry, but you need to go and tell your sister you need somewhere to stay.'

'You can't just chuck Will out, Auntie!' Charlie exploded.

'I'm not chucking him out. I'm sending him back to his family where he belongs.'

'What if his sister is still in hospital?'

'Then I'm sure the hospital will help make arrangements for Will's safety.'

Too stunned to speak, Will just stood looking at the house.

'Wait here. I'll see if it's safe to go back in,' Auntie said, picking her way through the rubble.

Frank walked over to Will. 'Why don't you come with us? I'm sure we can slip you on the train somewhere. There's bound to be someone who doesn't show.'

'Thanks, but I'm going to go back to the storeroom and try to get home. I know where it is now.'

Frank's face palled. 'You can't, Will. It's far too dangerous on your own.'

'I have to.' Will glared back at Frank. 'It will still be dangerous if you came with me. Anyway,' he added, 'it's not like a have any choice now, is it, with you off to the country?'

Charlie walked over. 'Come on, pal, come with us. 'I'm sure it won't be for long.'

'Thanks, guys, but I have to try, OK?' Will hunched his shoulders and walked up what was left of the path towards the house.

The atmosphere in the bedroom was tense as the boys packed their knapsacks. Auntie had told them they were not allowed anything other then their clothes, facecloth, toothbrush, towel and comb. Frank and Charlie, quiet for once, were nervous about leaving for the country and worried about Will leaving.

'Ready?' Frank said.

'Ready,' Charlie replied.

'Come on then.' Frank headed downstairs for the last time. Downstairs Auntie fussed around, handing them their gas masks and paper parcels containing bread and butter for their journey.

'Here's one for you, Will,' she said. 'I hope you find your sister much improved.'

'Thanks,' muttered Will, stuffing the package into his bag. He was sure he wouldn't want it; his stomach was in too many knots. *Anyway*, he thought, *I might be home in time for tea.*

Charlie pulled Will into a hug. 'Take care, pal.' His voice cracked.

Will hugged him back, fighting off the tears. He hadn't been here long, but they had been good friends to him.

Frank looped his arm around Will's neck and punched his arm playfully.

'It's been great having you to stay, chum.'

'Thanks for having me. I'll never forget you. And thank you, Auntie Doris, for feeding me,' Will said with a gulp.

'Get on with you.' She ruffled his hair. 'Safe journey, Will.'

Will walked away quickly before his nerves got the better of him and he begged Auntie to let them all stay.

Alone again in the city, Will felt afraid. He still couldn't get used to the devastation in every street, the taste of dirt and the smell of dust and powdered brickwork, or the constant fear that at any moment a German plane might fly over dropping more bombs on innocent people, him included.

He picked his way back to the site of the shop, his shoes crunching on the broken glass under his feet. It seemed to take a long time without Frank and Charlie by his side jostling with each other. He hoped they were OK.

He stopped briefly and looked around as if expecting to see them. Sighing he trudged on. As he got closer to the site, he could see that it was barricaded with bits of hastily nailed-together wood.

Panicking he ran the last few yards. The shop was totally cut off. There was no way he could get in. There wasn't even a small gap he could squeeze through.

Will felt faint. He sank down onto the ground. This could not be happening. Now what would he do?

He shut his eyes and tried to slow his breathing. He would look again for a way in. Opening his eyes he shakily lent on the wood, narrowly avoiding a splinter. He looked carefully at every brick in case there was a gap he had missed.

Nope, nothing. He had to make a plan. *Should he hang around in London waiting for Jim to come back?* He shook his head. That would mean living on the streets. He shuddered at the thought. But what then?

'Go and find Frank and Charlie,' came a distant voice. It was Jim! He jerked around looking for him.

'Jim?' he shouted. 'Jim!' There was no sign of him. He took off his glasses and wiped the dust from the lens. Maybe it was a sign? His mother was a great believer in signs.

He called out to a passer-by. 'Excuse me. Could you give me directions to the train station please?'

'Not running away, are you?' The gentleman laughed throatily.

'No, no, sir,' Will said with a slight stutter in his voice.

'That's OK then.' He blew slowly on his pipe before pointing Will in the right direction.

He would have to hurry if he was going to catch the boys. Fortunately the gentleman had told him a shortcut: down an alley, as long as it hadn't been bombed. Will went as quickly as he could. *I'm coming, Frank and Charlie, wait for me,* he repeated over and over in his head.

– CHAPTER ELEVEN–

The Evacuation

Will looked around the crowded platform. Children were crying and hanging on to their mothers' coats. Mothers were crying too. It was a dreadful symphony of noise, snot and tears. Suitcases and bags lay scattered over the platform, and the screech from the approaching train was deafening. Will had never seen a real steam train. It bore down on the platform like a fire-breathing dragon.

His eyes traced the length of the carriage. He couldn't believe all these children were being sent away. He had learned about evacuation in school, but he'd never imagined what it was truly like. Opening the door, he hopped into the carriage. Now all he had to do was find Frank and Charlie. He waited until the train had pulled out of the station before walking down the aisle looking from side to side for his friends. After three carriages he became worried. Surely they were on the train. He walked through to the last carriage, his heart hammering. Just as he was nearing the middle he saw them up ahead. He noticed their turned-down mouths, their newly-washed faces against the dusty window. Frank's fists were balled in his lap, whilst Charlie twisted a hanky round and round his fingers.

'Guess who,' he said, leaning over the back of their seats.

'Will!' they shouted simultaneously. 'What are you doing here?'

'The shop was all barricaded. There was no chance of me getting through. I'll have to go back in a week or so and try again with Jim,' he said, trying to make light of it.

They squeezed up to make room for him.

'That's if we ever get back.' Charlie looked glum. He started to draw patterns on the steamed up window with his finger.

'We will,' Will said, with more bravado than he felt.

They fell silent. Will wondered how he could cheer them up. He wracked his brain to think of something from the future that would amuse them.

'Have I told you about the time I tried skateboarding?' The boys turned from the window. Hurriedly he went on before they lost interest. 'It was a craze. Everyone had one, but it wasn't as easy as it looked,' he said.

'What's a skateboard?' Charlie interrupted.

'It's like a plank of wood with four wheels underneath,' Will said. 'You put one foot on and push off with the other. You can go really fast and do stunts and everything!'

'Could you do stunts?' asked Frank.

Will laughed. 'Well, no, I wasn't very good. In fact, I twisted my ankle and had to go to hospital. Mum was really cross.'

'Wow, I'm gonna make one!' Charlie said.

The rest of the journey was spent discussing skateboards and how they could get hold of some wheels to try and make one. Finally they arrived at the station, hungry and tired.

'Everybody on the buses. Hurry now!' announced a stern-looking man.

The boys quickly found themselves some seats on the

bus.

''Ere, mister, where are we going now?' Charlie asked.

'Village hall,' came the curt reply.

The twins made a face behind his back. They were past caring – as long as there was some food and a comfy bed at the end of it. Some of the other children weren't so relaxed. There was a low throb of sobbing coming from the back of the bus throughout the journey.

At the hall they were told to line up against the wall, girls on one side and boys on the other.

'What happens now?' Will asked the twins grumpily. He was beginning to wish he hadn't decided to follow them. He didn't get a reply.

He soon found out. Men and women were invited into the hall and asked which children they would like to look after. They walked up and down, scrutinizing the children's faces and sometimes checking their nails, muttering about worms and filth. When they were finally satisfied, they picked a boy or girl and the billet officer signed the child over to them. Most of the small children were picked first. It was like being auctioned off. Charlie and Frank noticed that some of the other brothers and sisters had been separated. They looked at each other, white-faced.

'Don't let them split us up, Frank,' pleaded Charlie.

'I won't!' promised Frank, looping his arm tightly around Charlie's shoulders. He puffed out his chest. 'I'll soon tell 'em.'

Will blinked nervously. He knew it was unlikely that whoever took the twins would take him as well, but he decided to ask one of the billeting officers anyway.

'Excuse me?' He tugged the lady's sleeve. 'I'm an orphan, but I live with Frank and Charlie here.' He pointed to them. 'So do you think we might all go together?'

The billeting officer didn't meet Will's eye. 'I doubt that very much, lad,' she said.

Will's bottom lip began to tremble. His jaw set and he clenched his fists. *I will not cry*, he said to himself.

'We will try and keep you in the same village. That's the best I can do,' she said.

At that moment a short, stocky, good-humoured man with a neat moustache walked over to the twins. 'I'll take these two,' he said. 'Wife always wanted twins.'

'Can I come too, sir?' Will stepped forward.

'No, sorry, lad, we've only enough room for two.'

Charlie and Frank just had time to shake Will's hand quickly before they were marched off.

'Don't worry, Will, we'll find you!' shouted Frank as they trailed out the door.

Before Will had a chance to wave goodbye, the billeting officer grabbed his arm. 'Come on,' she said. 'I've managed to persuade Samuel Drey to take you in. He has a farm just outside the village where the twins will be staying.'

Will went to meet him. 'Pleased to meet you, sir,' he said, holding his hand out. 'Thanks for taking me in.'

Both Will and his outstretched hand were ignored. Instead Farmer Drey thrust Will out of the building and up to a waiting horse and cart.

'Get in,' he said brusquely.

Will climbed up, trying not to put too much weight on his ankle; it still ached a bit. He looked sideways at Farmer Drey as the horse cantered along. He had large hands with short stubby nails. His shirt was pulled tightly across broad shoulders. A hat was wedged low over his forehead so that it rested on his intensely black eyebrows. Will decided he didn't look very friendly.

They jolted along narrow lanes that twisted and turned. Will clung onto the side of the cart, convinced that he would fall out at any moment.

'How much further is it?' he said with a squeak.

Farmer Drey glanced at him. 'Not far,' he said tersely.

'It must be nice living in the country,' Will said, trying to make conversation.

''Tis hard work. Just because you're a city boy don't think you can sit about idle all day.'

Will gave up. He hoped that Mrs Drey might be more pleasant, although he didn't plan on staying in the country long enough to find out.

– CHAPTER TWELVE –

Life on the Farm

Will and Farmer Drey arrived at the farmhouse. A large shaggy sheepdog ran out to greet them, barking loudly. Will pressed his back against the cart and hoped the dog was friendlier than he sounded.

'Be quiet, Max!' roared Farmer Drey, forcing the dog out of the way with his knee.

He led Will into a warm kitchen. 'This is Mrs Drey. Make sure you mind your P's and Q's when speaking to her.'

Mrs Drey was short and round with small beady eyes and freckles around her button nose. She smiled at Will. He instantly felt comforted and smiled back at her friendly face.

'Pleased to meet you,' she said. She seemed to sense Will's uneasiness. 'Sit down, lad, I've made you some stew. There's plenty of bread and butter. I expect you're starving after all that travelling.' She quickly ladled a bowl of stew and put it in front of Will. It smelled incredible, although it did look a bit watery. There were even chunks of meat nestled amongst the turnips and potatoes.

Will was indeed famished. 'Thanks,' he said, as he took a chunk of bread and dipped it into the bowl.

'Tuck in. Then I'll show you your room.' Mrs Drey placed a cup of tea in front of him. He hadn't liked tea before this adventure started, but he was getting a taste for it. Well, he didn't seem to have much choice; there was nothing else on offer it would seem.

Mr Drey snorted. 'I'm off to check the animals,' he said, banging the door shut behind him. Will heard him yelling for Max. *Poor dog*. His thoughts turned to Rollo sitting at home waiting for him. He winced and shook his head, making a mental effort to dislodge the thought. He had to stay strong.

Will sat in silence and ate his stew while Mrs Drey tidied up the kitchen. It was much larger than Frank and Charlie's house. It had a stone floor with a big black range cooker along one side. The kitchen table took up most of the centre of the room. There was a rocking chair in one corner, from which a rather bedraggled-looking cat eyed the newcomer suspiciously.

'Thank you, Mrs Drey, that was really lovely,' Will said. 'It's very kind of you to put me up.'

Mrs Drey seemed delighted at his response to her stew. 'Come on. Let's get you to bed. You will have a busy day tomorrow helping Mr Drey. Just remember, do what he says. And don't mind his harsh words. He doesn't mean no harm by them. He works hard and it's a tough business, farming. As you'll no doubt find out soon enough.'

Will nodded, yawning.

Mrs Drey led him upstairs to a small back room. 'Here you are then. I've cleared a couple of drawers for you,' she said. 'Remember not to open the curtains. We don't want any of those nasty German bombs falling on us.'

Will sat on the bed and looked around his new room. It was very dark, even with the light on. There was a bed, a chair, a chest of drawers. The room was freezing. Will decided not to bother getting undressed – it was too cold – and dived beneath the covers. Tomorrow I'm going to tell Frank and Charlie I'm going back to London as soon as I can.

He was asleep in minutes.

'Will, Will, wake up,' Mrs Drey said, giving him a shake. 'I've brought you some tea.'

'What time is it?' Will mumbled.

Mrs Drey set his tea down on the chair next to his bed and opened his curtains. 'Six thirty. Now come on, be quick. Mr Drey is waiting for you.'

Will pulled back the bedspread. Mrs Drey gave a tutting noise when she saw he was still wearing his clothes from the day before. Not fully awake, he pulled on his shoes and stumbled downstairs, where Mrs Drey was waiting for him, bacon roll in one hand and a jacket in the other.

'Here, put this on. It will keep the chill out. You'll find Mr Drey over in the big barn.' She held the door open, letting the fresh morning air inside.

Will strolled over to the barn, savouring his roll. Bacon butties had never tasted this good back home.

'Get a move on, lad!' shouted Mr Drey, as soon as he

spotted him. 'These cows won't clean themselves out. Here, take these.' He held out a shovel and a stiff broom. 'Just sweep it all through. I've got milking to do. I'll be back in a bit to see how you're doing… no slacking, mind.' He stomped off, his wellies oozing a trail of muck in his wake.

Will looked down at the barn floor. It was matted with old straw, mud and poo. It stank.

Hunching his shoulders, he used the back of the shovel to scrape the floor. *How surprised would Grandad be if he could see me now?*

A tear dropped off the end of his chin, surprising him as it melted into the messy floor. He hadn't felt the tears begin, but now they had started, he couldn't seem to stop them. If only he could close his eyes and be back home.

Mucking out the cows' barn kept him busy and warm for a good few hours. Before now, the closest he'd got to a cow was driving past fields of them as his mum's car sped along the motorway. The black and white beasts blinked at Will. 'You know I'm not supposed to be here,' Will said, patting the warm flank of the nearest cow. *Who'd have thought I'd end up talking to a herd of cows?* Their soft mooing lulled him into a cosy daydream. It was shattered by the familiar voice of Farmer Drey.

'Haven't you finished that yet, lad?'

'Nearly,' Will mumbled.

'I need your help on the top field. One of the animal shelters is broken. Come on, quick, quick.' He handed Will a hammer and some nails. 'You carry those, I'll get the wood. Meet me there in five minutes.'

Will trudged through the field, keeping an eye out for any sheep. They were in the next field and Will wasn't sure if they could get out. He had never trusted sheep ever since he had been on a picnic with his cousins. One minute they were alone in a field and the next they were being chased by a gang of angry ewes. One had even tried to bite him as he flung himself over the gate.

Mr Drey arrived shortly after Will. 'Bang a nail in here,' he said, placing a piece of wood over the broken board.

Will tapped it with the hammer. The nail wouldn't go in. He tried again, hitting it a bit harder. It still wouldn't go in.

'Give it here, boy! Good grief, where are your

muscles?' He grabbed the hammer from Will, slamming it into the nail. 'That should do it,' he grunted. 'Right let's have a quick look at the fence.' He marched off. Will traipsed behind. He missed the warmth of the barn, even with that potent smell. They walked in silence to the far corner of the field.

'Thought so. It's rotten at the bottom. We need to fix that or the sheep will soon be able to push their way through. Wait here, lad. I need to go back to the barn for a couple of tools.'

Will was dog-tired. He waited until Mr Drey was out of sight before lying back on the grass, enjoying the fresh air. The wind puffed the clouds as they scudded across the sky. The sun had fully risen now. Its heat had begun to soak into the grass and found its way to Will's weary bones. He closed his eyes and let his mind drift.

'Hello.'

Startled, Will's eyes snapped open and he sat up. There in front of him stood a tall, skinny girl with freckles and long ginger pigtails. She was wearing dungarees; her shirtsleeves didn't quite reach her wrists. She looked about his age.

'I've brought you some lunch,' she said, holding out a paper bag.

'Err, thanks,' Will said. 'I'm Will, by the way.'

'Yes, I know. Mrs Drey told me. I'm Elizabeth. I help out here on the weekends. You're an evacuee, aren't you?'

'Yes, I arrived yesterday from London. My mates came too, but they're in the village somewhere,' he said glumly.

'I live in the village.' Elizabeth played with her pigtails. 'Were you bombed in London?'

'Yeah,' Will said, taking a bite from the sandwich. The bread was cut in doorstop-thick slices. It was just what he needed.

'Crikey, that must have been scary!'

'Scary, smelly, hot, noisy and dirty,' Will said.

'You'll enjoy it here then,' Elizabeth said, sitting down and pushing her fringe out of her eyes. 'We haven't been bombed at all. It's very quiet in these parts.'

'Where exactly are we?' Will said. 'I couldn't see much in the dark when we arrived.'

'Shirehampton, near Bristol. Why?'

'No reason, just wondered how far we'd come. It

seemed to take forever to get here.' Will munched his apple thoughtfully. 'I wish I could go to the village now and see how my friends are getting on.'

'You'll see them at school soon enough.'

Will frowned. He had forgotten all about school. 'Will you be there?'

'Oh yes, it's great fun. We have lessons in the morning, and in the afternoons we do stuff for the war effort.' Elizabeth stood up. 'I'd better get back. Mrs Drey will wonder where I've got to. See you Monday,' she called as she skipped away. Her cheerful tones had definitely brightened up the day. Will felt almost happy.

By mid-afternoon, however, Will had had enough. He wasn't used to heavy work, and it felt like he had walked miles, trailing back and forth, back and forth, across muddy fields.

'Come on, lad. You town boys need to toughen up,' Mr Drey said. 'Nothing like the great outdoors to make a man out of you.'

Will just nodded. He had been listening to comments like that all day. It was pointless trying to argue. Finally, as the sun set, Mr Drey said they had finished and it was time for supper.

Will collapsed gratefully onto the kitchen chair.

'Here you are, then.' Mrs Drey placed a plate in front of him. 'Rabbit pie.'

Will turned green. He wasn't sure he could eat rabbit – what if it made him sick? He tentatively took a bite. It wasn't as bad as he thought it would be. He was still reluctant to eat it, but one look at Mr Drey's scowl showed him that refusal wasn't an option. He would just have to try and pretend it was something else… chicken stew, maybe.

Will lay in bed thinking about Jim. Was he really his dad? Will hadn't mentioned this to Charlie and Frank. He didn't know why really. Perhaps it might change things between them. Plus he had no way of knowing if it were true.

Suddenly he sat up. What if he could persuade Jim to go back the future with him? He had to think of a way to get back to London!

– CHAPTER THIRTEEN –

The Stash

'You can sweep the yard this morning, lad. Mrs Drey and I are going to church. That should keep you out of trouble. And make sure you do a thorough job.' Mr Drey pointed his spoon at Will, egg running down his chin.

After they left, Will wondered around the farmhouse. It wasn't very homely. There was sparse furniture and no books or photographs on display. After helping himself to another cup of tea, Will drifted out into the yard to start sweeping before they came back. He didn't want to get balled out again.

Opening the shed door, Will looked for the yard broom and some gloves. There was so much stuff crammed in it was hard to see. He took an old blanket from the shelf and his eyes nearly popped out of his head; lying on the shelf underneath were open boxes of chocolates, tinned food and cigarettes. *What on earth were they doing in there?* He knew from his time in London that chocolate was rationed. Hastily Will covered it back up again – but not before shoving a bar or two of chocolate in his pockets for his friends. He was sure that Mr Drey wouldn't want him knowing he'd found it. Grabbing the broom, he hastily closed the shed door.

'Oi! You boy! Where is Samuel Drey?' hollered a voice. Will jumped, but then composed himself, leaning on the broom as he stared at the visitor. The man had a wide-brimmed hat perched on his head; his light-coloured suit didn't fit very well, and he wore a brightly coloured tie. He walked right up to Will and offered an insincere smile. He had a little pencil moustache which creased as he talked. 'Well? Where is he?'

Will didn't like the sound of his voice. He took a step back. 'If you mean Farmer Drey then he's out.'

'Just you tell him that Mr Birch is looking for him.'

'OK.' Will started to sweep again, hoping that the man would just leave.

Leaning over, the man grabbed the broom handle from Will, causing him to stumble and threw it onto the ground. 'And don't you forget, sonny.' He turned on his heel and walked swiftly away.

'I see you swept the yard, boy.' Farmer Drey sat back in his chair and scratched his plump stomach.

'Yes,' Will replied sourly. 'Thank you for a lovely lunch, Mrs Drey,' he added. 'Oh, Mr Drey, I almost forgot. A man was looking for you this morning. He said that his name was Mr Birch and that he will be back. Actually he looked a bit cross.'

Mr Drey leapt out of his chair, and grabbed Will by his shirt collar. 'What did you tell him?' he said, his face slowly going puce and spittle forming at the corners of his mouth.

'Er, I said, um… I said I would give you the message.' Will wriggled in Mr Drey's vice-like grip.

'Upstairs with you. Go on.' Mr Drey shoved Will towards the stairs. 'And don't come back down tonight, no supper for you boy, that'll teach you.'

'But—'

'Just go, Will.' Mrs Drey's voice was soft.

Will stomped up the stairs, wondering what on earth

he had done wrong. He kicked off his shoes and flung himself on the bed. Grabbing a chocolate bar from under mattress, he decided the sooner he left the country the better. The food might be better but clearly the people weren't.

The next morning Mrs Drey handed Will a paper bag. 'I've made you some sandwiches and an apple for school. It's in the village. Over there.' She opened the back door and pointed. 'Hurry now,' she said. 'You don't want to be late on your first day.'

Will opened his mouth to argue but then thought better of it. He'd rather be in school with Frank and Charlie than on the farm with psycho Mr Drey.

The path to the village was narrow, with tall hedgerows on each side. The road was deserted. Will soon found the school and decided to wait outside for Charlie and Frank. He spotted them as they walked around the corner chatting.

'Hi, Will!' they shouted, running over to greet him.

'How's it going?' Charlie asked.

'OK, I guess. I've been working on the farm all

weekend.' He kicked a stone viciously. 'How about you two? What have you been up to?'

'Oh, it's top notch, isn't it, Frank?' Charlie beamed. 'We are being treated like kings. Great grub, new clothes, comfy beds.'

Frank looked at Will's grumpy face. 'Sure, but I bet being on a farm is fun too! All that space to play in.'

'And smelly animals to clean out,' grumbled Will.

'Hi, Will!'

Will turned around to see Elizabeth standing shyly behind him. 'Hi, Elizabeth. This is Charlie and Frank.'

'Hello!' the boys replied as one.

They walked into the playground, dodging the children playing with hoops and balls. Before Will could pick up the conversation where they left off, the teacher came out of the school clanging a large-handled bell.

– CHAPTER FOURTEEN–

Starting School

'Line up! Line up!' the teacher shouted.

In military fashion the children were marched into school. Will was surprised to find there was only one classroom. The desks were joined together and there weren't enough seats for everyone. Will sniffed. The classroom smelled musty and felt damp. There were posters on the walls, reminding children what to do in an air raid, as well as pictures of the King and Winston Churchill.

'Come on, children, settle down,' said the teacher. 'Find yourself a place to sit. Little ones, come here in front, you will have to sit on the mat. Older children can share desks at the back. For our new arrivals my name is Miss Richards. I hope you will be made very welcome in our village. Now, let's all stand for morning prayers. Hands together and bow your heads.'

They recited the Lord's Prayer. Will stumbled through the words, but everyone else seemed to know them by heart. Next, they all sang *There'll Always Be An England*. Will didn't know the words, so he opened and shut his mouth like a goldfish, hoping he was in time with the other children. When they finished, the teacher gave them all some paper from an exercise book and a pen that you dipped into an inkwell. Will found this quite difficult to use. *I wish I'd brought my biro*, he thought.

'Those of you who are new, I would like you to write a short paragraph about yourself and your family back home. The rest of you can write about what you did at the weekend.'

Will smiled to himself. He'd better just write about staying with Frank and Charlie, he supposed. Nobody would believe anything else, especially if he wrote about his classroom back home, furnished with smartboards and laptops.

Charlie and Frank started squabbling.

'Hey! You're writing the same stuff as me,' Frank complained, covering his page with his arm.

'But I live in the same house as you, so it would be

the same, dummy!' Charlie answered back.

'*So?* Write about something else!' Frank said peevishly.

Charlie rolled his eyes and tried to pry Frank's arm away from his paper. Miss Richards came hurrying over to see what the row was about.

'You can both write about home,' she said firmly. 'I'm sure you can think of different things to say, even if you are twins.'

'Hmm, suppose,' Charlie said, nibbling the edge of his finger, already covered in blue ink.

Elizabeth watched the squabbling with an amused smile. 'My dad was helping load supplies for the soldiers,' she said to Will.

'What does he do?' Will asked.

'He's a manager at the dockyard. He oversees all the ships coming in and out.'

'Heads down now, children,' Miss Richards ordered.

The rest of the morning passed by peacefully and it was soon lunchtime.

'This afternoon the nit nurse is coming to check your

heads,' Miss Richards said as the children filed out. 'So if you go home for lunch, give your hair a good brushing.'

Will sat down with the twins to eat their sandwiches.

'What's it really like up at the farm then?' Charlie asked Will.

'Well, actually...' Will paused and looked around, making sure no one else was listening. 'I made a discovery!'

'What? What?' Charlie dropped his sandwich in excitement.

'Mr Drey left me alone yesterday—'

'Yes!' Charlie leaned forward on his knees.

'I had to sweep out the yard, and when I went into the shed to fetch the broom you'll never guess what I found!'

'A body?' joked Frank.

'A stash.'

'A stash?' Frank looked puzzled.

'Yes.' Will huddled in closer to the boys. 'A stash of chocolate, cigarettes and tins of food! What do you make of that then?'

'I bet he's a spiv, or a go-between.' Frank looked at

Charlie. 'Remember old lightfingers down our street. He was always floggin' stuff.'

'Yeah, I remember.'

'What's a spiv?' asked Will.

'Really? Blimey! A Spiv buys and sells stuff on the black market. I reckon the farm is just a front,' Frank said.

'That's probably why Farmer Drey was so touchy when this bloke came sniffing around the farm.' Will bit into his apple letting the juice run down his hand.

'You need to be careful, Will,' Frank said. 'You don't want to be caught up with a load of crooks.'

Miss Richards came out and rang the bell for afternoon school. The boys all stood up.

'I nicked you some chocolate,' Will said, as the three boys lined up for their hair to be checked. 'I'll give it to you at home time.'

The nit nurse sat on a chair at the front of the class and checked each child's scalp in turn. Will was relieved to find he didn't have nits!

'I'll walk back with you, Will. I live at the end of the village,' Elizabeth said when class was dismissed for the day. 'It was great hearing all your stories,' she added as they strolled along the lane.

'Just as well I didn't tell you the truth,' Will muttered under his breath.

Elizabeth stopped walking. 'Pardon?'

'Oh nothing.' Will continued striding up the road.

Elizabeth skipped to keep pace with him. 'You know, you talk a bit different from the others,' she said.

Will halted and stared at her. 'I can't help that, can I?' he said, and stomped off.

'Well I never!' Elizabeth said to no one in particular.

Will was cross with himself. It was silly of him to get angry with Elizabeth. It wasn't her fault. She didn't know about his secret. He was supposed to be making friends, not losing them.

– CHAPTER FIFTEEN–

The Lost Sheep

A few days later Mr Drey said he needed Will's help. 'No school today, I need you here.'

'I can help when I get home,' Will said. 'My friends are at school.'

Mr Drey swung round and clouted Will around the ear.

'Ow!' Will yelped, jumping back.

'Let's get this straight,' Mr Drey said,'when I tell you to do something, that's what you do! I don't take cheek from a boy.'

Will raised his hand to his ear tentatively. It hurt. But he didn't dare cry. What was happening? No one had ever hit him before.

'OK,' he said, quietly, rubbing his sore ear.

'What did you say?' Mr Drey barked back.

'I said OK, er, sir,' Will replied, afraid of getting a

second thumping.

He spent the day helping Mr Drey repair one of the low fences. A sheep had tried to get out and become stuck in the wire.

Eventually he plucked up the courage to ask the question that had been on his mind all day. 'Can I go to school tomorrow?'

'Yes, lad.' Mr Drey's bad mood seemed to have passed. He was even whistling while he worked.

So what had made him so cross earlier? Will wondered if it was something to do with the spiv.

The next day he mentioned it to Charlie and Frank.

'I wouldn't worry, chum,' Frank said. 'Our dad used to cuff us all the time. Didn't he, Charlie?'

'Yeah, and it flippin' hurt sometimes,' Charlie said. 'He said we drove him barmy.'

'Hmm,' replied Will. 'Parents aren't supposed to hit their children in the future.'

'Really?' Charlie couldn't hide his amazement. 'Well, how do the kids know if they have done wrong then?'

Will shrugged. 'Never really thought about it. They just do, I guess.'

*

Elizabeth caught up with Will on the way home. 'How is it going at the farm?' she asked.

'Alright, I suppose,' replied Will stiffly. His tone softened. 'Sorry about marching off the other day. I just want to go back to London.'

'That's OK. I know Mr Drey can be a bit sharp at times. Best to keep your head down and do what he says. I'm sure you'll love it here when you get used to it.'

Will didn't see the point in arguing with her.

By the end of the week Will's mood had sunk to new depths. He saw less and less of Charlie and Frank. They would hang out with the children on their street. Will couldn't do this as he was tied to the farm. Mr Drey had told him that he was not allowed friends back to play, and no one seemed in any great hurry to return to London. When he had asked the twins if they had heard from their auntie, they simply said she was fine, and the house was taking a while to get repaired.

'Just enjoy yourself here for a while, Will,' said Frank. 'Can't see the rush to get back myself.' He seemed to have totally forgotten that 'getting back' held a very different meaning for Will.

Will was helping Mr Drey move the sheep from one field to the next when Elizabeth came running up, red-faced and panting.

'Quickly, Mr Drey! Mrs Drey's had a funny turn. You need to come to the farmhouse!'

Mr Drey bolted out of the field, with Elizabeth racing along to keep up with him.

Will was left to round up the sheep. To his horror, as he counted them, he found he was one short. *Oh no! This isn't good. I'm done for now,* he thought. He felt beads of sweat form on his forehead. He tried not to panic.

He began to walk around the edge of the field to check if the sheep had got stuck in a ditch, but he couldn't see it anywhere. Perhaps it was still in the other field.

Just as he was closing the gate behind him, Mr Drey appeared with Max at his heels.

'Sheep all in?' he asked gruffly.

'Um, not quite,' stammered Will. 'I think one is missing.'

'Missing?' Mr Drey repeated the word like it was poisonous. 'Do you know how much they are worth? You're nothing but a useless city boy with a posh accent.' He grabbed Will's arm. 'Right, come with me.'

He dragged a terrified Will to an old shed in a corner of the field. Opening the door, he flung the boy inside. 'You can stay there till I see fit to let you out!' he said.

Will heard the lock click and the farmer's footsteps retreating. His heart raced and his breath escaped in small gasps. *What was happening?*

'Let me out! Let me out!' he shouted, banging on the door with his fist.

The shed smelled damp. Shadows loomed out of the darkness. He hammered on the door until his voice became hoarse and his hands bled. It was early evening and he could feel the darkness begin to deepen. Sucking in lungfuls of stagnant air, he tried to calm himself. Will hated confined spaces, always had, since the time his cousin had shut him in the wardrobe when he was six. He could vividly remember fighting the clothes and jackets, smelling his mother's perfume on every piece of fabric, terrified he would suffocate and no one would know.

Now, once again, he felt the walls closing in, sweat trickling down his back as the space shrank around him.

I've got to get out, but how?

His head throbbing, he stuck his arms out in front of his body and tried to trace his surroundings.

'Arghh!'

Will rubbed his hand over his face and swept away a sticky cobweb. His fingers felt something wooden. He ran his hand down the length of the item and felt prongs – a fork, maybe.

Perhaps he could bash the door open with it, or dig a hole underneath to lever the door.

He lifted the fork with both hands and jabbed it hard against the door, but it stood fast. Panting, he tried again. His fingers picked at the ground beneath his feet. It was just earth. There didn't seem to be a solid floor. With a bit of luck, he might be able to make0 a decent-sized hole and use the fork to prise open the door.

His fingers made contact with another object, something hard and smooth. Will examined it blindly. It was quite long, and knobbly at one end. He scrabbled in the dirt trying to get it out. With a mighty tug, it came free. He held it against the fading sunlight seeping through a knothole in the side of the shed and shrieked.

Instinctively, he threw the thing to the floor.

With revulsion he realised he had been holding a bone – a human bone. It could have been part of an arm or a leg! *What on earth has Mr Drey buried here? Has he killed someone?* He grabbed the fork and thrust it into the ground. He had to get out now. Before he had shifted more than three or four forkfuls of soil, the door flew open.

'Oh, poor you!' exclaimed Elizabeth, hugging him. 'Are you OK?' She stood back and looked at his dirty tear-stained face.

'Fine,' snapped Will, shoving her out of the way as he stumbled from the shed. Bending over, he put his hands on his knees and drank in mouthfuls of air, glad to be back out in the open. 'I like getting locked in sheds!' He glared at her.

'You ungrateful, hateful beast!' Elizabeth snapped, her eyes blazing. 'I wasn't the one who put you in there!'

Will sat down. His legs felt unsteady. 'How did you

know?' he said through gritted teeth.

'Mr Drey told Mrs Drey he'd shut you in to teach you a lesson, but she got cross with him and said he had to let you out, so he sent me.'

'I lost a sheep. That's why he locked me up,' Will said with a shudder. 'I don't think you should come here, Elizabeth. It's not safe.'

'What do you mean, not safe?'

'I found a bone in the shed. Mr Drey must have buried something here.' He whispered the words, although there was no one to overhear him.

'Really,' Elizabeth said wide-eyed. 'Let's see.'

Will led her back to the shed, dredging up the last of his courage to venture inside. 'Look!' he pointed to the bone lying on the floor.

Elizabeth took a step closer and squinted. 'It's an animal bone, silly!'

Will was stunned. 'How can you be sure?'

'I've seen them before. Nothing to worry about, Will, you daft thing.' She laughed and put her arm around his shoulder. She had clearly forgiven him for his earlier rudeness, but Will was now feeling very self-conscious about his over-reaction. An animal bone! Of course it was. How could he be so stupid?

He sniffed. 'Well, I don't like it here anyway. I'm leaving!'

'But you can't,' Elizabeth said. 'You've been billeted here. You can't just leave!'

'We'll see,' Will said. He'd never felt more determined about anything in his life.

Mrs Drey came to see him in bed that night.

'I'm sorry about Mr Drey,' she said. 'He is under a bit of strain at the moment. Money is a bit tight and we might lose the farm. He didn't mean to lock you up, I'm sure.'

Will stared at her. What *could* he say?

'I'll leave you to sleep now.' Mrs Drey shut the door softly behind her.

He thumped his fist on his pillow. 'I hate it here!' He spat the words out. 'Hate, hate, hate it!'

CHAPTER SIXTEEN

Elizabeth Knows

'I'm running away,' Will said, looking defiant. 'I don't care about the bombs anymore'

Elizabeth gasped. 'Running away!' she squealed. 'You can't, you'll get into so much trouble.'

'Not if they don't catch me,' Will said. 'Anyway, keep it to yourself. I don't want you telling anyone. I shouldn't have said anything.'

'Oh, Will.' Elizabeth sighed and then took his hand. 'Please think very carefully.'

Will shook his hand free. 'Come on.' He marched ahead. 'We'll be late.'

Mr Drey had given Will some time off, and they were meeting Charlie and Frank for a picnic. While they were eating, Will decided to tell the twins. 'I've had enough of Farmer Drey,' he said. 'So I'm leaving. You guys want to come with me?'

Frank looked amazed. 'Leaving?' he repeated.

'Leaving?' echoed Charlie.

'Yup. You in or not?'

'But how would we get back to London?' Frank asked.

'I don't know. Maybe we could flag down a car, get a lift?'

'No way, pal,' Frank said, shaking his head. 'Anyway, just how many cars do you think would be driving to London? None, that's how many.'

'What if we tried to hide in a train carriage?' Will had already given this idea some thought.

'It's too risky,' Frank said. 'Anyway, why go back when it's so much nicer here? You can almost taste the air. Just look up.' He tilted his head. 'Miles and miles of blue sky and clouds. It's birds what wakes us up 'ere not bombs. You 'aint gettin' that in London. Nah, Will, we don't want to go back to the hard cold streets. Sorry, you're on your own this time.'

'Have you forgotten *why* I need to go back to London?' Will raised his voice in exasperation.

'Course not, but I'm sure we'll go back eventually. Jim will still be there.' Frank tried to calm things down.

Elizabeth was giving them all funny looks. Some very awkward questions would be on the cards if Will didn't shut up.

Will shrugged. 'I had wondered about catching a lift with one of the supply ships that Elizabeth said are at the docks. They go to London. It can't be that hard.'

Elizabeth looked shocked. 'You can't do that, Will! It's very dangerous at the docks.'

'Sounds dodgy to me. What if you get there and there ain't any ships in? You'll have to come back here and face the Dreys,' Frank said.

'No way,' Will said. 'I would hitch a lift or something. Do you want to come or not?'

'Nah, we like it here, don't we?' Charlie looked at Frank. 'And Auntie says the raids are getting more frequent. We would be in danger. Anyway the grub's better here.' Charlie shoved a sandwich in his mouth as if to prove a point.

'I'm not staying here to be locked in a shed over and over again.' Will felt deflated at his friend's lack of enthusiasm to join him. 'And I'm not going to another home either.' He stuck his jaw out. 'If you don't want to come with me then I'll go alone.'

He strode off, seething with disappointment and frustration. Elizabeth got up to follow him, but Frank yanked her back down. 'Leave him. He'll come round, you'll see.'

Charlie wasn't so sure and neither was Elizabeth. She set off after Will, full of questions that needed answers.

Elizabeth appeared panting alongside him. 'Will, wait!' She clutched her side, puffing and gasping. 'Please stay… at least for a few more days while you think about this.'

'I can't.' Will looked into her eyes. 'Elizabeth, will you help me?'

She twiddled her hair around her finger and looked at him thoughtfully.

'I don't know, Will. I don't think you should run away.'

'Please, can you just ask your dad for the name of any ships that go to London?'

'I could *try*,' Elizabeth said reluctantly. 'But won't that be top secret?'

'Just say it's a project we're doing at school. We have to think of names for ships, and you wondered if he knew any. *Please!* I don't fit in here. I want to see my grandad.' Will's face crumpled. 'You guys have been great. I don't know what I would have done without you, but I *have* to get home.'

Elizabeth walked back to meet Charlie and Frank. The mood was sombre as they wended their way home.

Charlie turned to Elizabeth. 'We've got a secret,' he blurted.

'Oh tell me,' Elizabeth said. 'I love secrets and never let on, I promise.'

Frank jabbed Charlie, causing him to stumble. 'You're not going to tell her about Will, are you?'

Charlie's eyes gleamed, 'Come on, buddy, you've got to admit it's a great secret. Will needs all the help he can get right now.'

'What *is* it?' Elizabeth squealed, hopping up and down on one foot. '*Please* tell me.'

Frank looked around the field, checking they couldn't be overheard. 'The thing is…' he said with a long pause.

'Yes?' Elizabeth looked like she might burst at any minute.

'The thing is…' he repeated. 'Will is from the future.'

'The future?' Elizabeth said, looking blankly at him. 'But I don't understand. How can he be? What do you mean the future?'

'He's a time traveller,' Charlie said importantly.

'A time traveller?' Elizabeth shook her head. 'I don't believe you. You're making it up. Honestly, boys are the *worst*...'

''S the truth,' Charlie said, offended. 'He came through a time hole and now he's stuck here.'

'It was our job to help him find it, but then we were bombed out and evacuated,' Frank said.

'He's got this really swell thing too,' Charlie said. 'He calls it a mobile phone. It has pictures on it and everything.'

Frank scowled at him. 'Sshh, Charlie. Elizabeth doesn't need to know that.'

Elizabeth clasped her hands together. 'Time traveller,' she said breathlessly. 'Wow, just *wow!*' She drifted off for a moment, then added, 'Poor Will!' She slumped down on the grass. 'No wonder he seems so cross and lonely sometimes.'

'You mustn't say we told you,' Frank said, glaring at

Elizabeth. 'Only we gave our word, see.'

The following day Elizabeth waited for Will outside the school gate. Before he could even say 'Hello', she grabbed him and dragged him to a quiet corner of the playground.

'I spoke to my dad,' she said, unable to hide her excitement. 'He says there are a couple of ships that stop at his dock that are named after Greek gods, like Aristotle and Poseidon, I can't remember exactly. I asked if they went to London. He said that was top secret, but they picked up supplies from around the country. He says it is quite possible that they do. You could try and get on one. They leave early in the morning. I know that because Dad has to leave before we get up.'

Will couldn't believe it – his first bit of luck in days. 'Wow! Thank you, Elizabeth! I had a quick look at Mr Drey's atlas the other night. It's about ten miles, I think. If I left when they were asleep, I could just about walk it in time.'

'I could lend you my bike. You'll get there much quicker.'

'But then your bike would be lost. I don't want to get

you into trouble.' Will looked worried.

'Don't worry, I'll think of something,' Elizabeth said, cocking her head. 'I'll say I lent it to a friend.'

Will couldn't help himself and hugged her. 'Thanks,' he said, grinning. 'You're the best!'

Elizabeth's face turned red. 'Just make sure you write to me then,' she said, forgetting that it would be impossible once her new friend returned to the future.

– CHAPTER SEVENTEEN–

The Escape

Will was ready to leave. He had put some fruit, bread and cheese and a flask of tea in a bag. All that remained to do was sit tight until the Dreys were asleep, and then he would make his escape.

To keep himself awake, he sat on the edge of his bed and read a book. It was hard to concentrate on the pages, and the words faded before him as his mind focused on the journey ahead.

Finally, quietness settled on the house. Will looked at his watch. It was a quarter past eleven. He had plenty of time to get to the docks.

The window creaked as he opened it and cautiously climbed out onto the ledge. The moon was bright, helping him locate the drainpipe easily. He bottom-shuffled along the ledge, moving inch by inch until he could stretch across and grab the pipe. He only hoped it would take his weight. He took a deep breath, wrapped his arms around it and pushed himself off the ledge. He shimmied down until, at last, he felt solid ground under his feet.

Will let out the breath he had been holding and stood listening for Max. A barn owl hooted, startling him as it flew past. He crept out of the yard and began to walk briskly to the village to pick up Elizabeth's bike.

It didn't take him long to reach her house. The handlebars of her bike were sticking out of the hedge. He dragged it out from its hiding place. There was a note stuck on the saddle.

Dearest Will,

I hope you arrive safely in London. I will be thinking about you and hope you find time before you leave to write that you are safe and well. Don't worry about the bike.

Godspeed, Elizabeth.

Will folded the letter carefully and put it at the bottom of his bag. He removed the chocolate he had taken from the shed, and he placed it under the hedge, where he hoped Elizabeth would find it.

He hopped on to the bike and pedalled fiercely. Adrenaline kept his legs pumping, but after an hour of hard peddling he was tired and thirsty. He glanced at his watch and decided it was time for a short break. He rested the bike on the grass verge, scrambled up to the top, sat down and rummaged in his bag for his flask. The tea was refreshing. Lying back to look at the stars, Will allowed himself time to dwell on his adventure. He could still hardly believe what had happened to him. Children in 1943 had a hard life; his experiences here had certainly toughened him up. An image of Charlie and Frank laughing and shoving each other playfully drifted into his mind, and he wondered how much he'd miss them when he got home. He decided he'd try harder to make friends in future. The night air was soft and sweet with the first scents of autumn. Within minutes he was asleep.

He woke with a start. A man was prodding him repeatedly. 'Can't stay here, lad.'

Will looked up, his eyes taking in the uniform of a soldier wearing a tin helmet and an armband that read Home Guard.

'Come on, I'll see you back home,' the man said,

pulling Will up.

'I can find my own way.' Will wriggled out of his grip.

'Look, lad, it's late and dark. You shouldn't be out here by yourself.'

Will grabbed his bag and tried to make a run for it.

'Oh no you don't! Any more of this behaviour and you'll be accompanying me to the police station.'

'Sorry, sir, you just startled me. Please let me go. I'll go straight home. Look, I've got my bike.'

'What I want to know is what you're doing out here in the first place?'

Will thought quickly. 'Well, I just thought it would be exciting. Cycling in the dark. Bit of an adventure and all that.' He looked at his feet, his voice petering out.

'You won't think it's exciting if the bombs start to fall. Go on then, get off home with you. Don't let me catch you again.'

'Thanks, sir.'

Will grabbed the bike and peddled away, avoiding the temptation to look back at the man. A mile down the road, he stopped and looked at his watch; the colour drained from his face. He might not have enough time.

Stupid, stupid, falling asleep like that, he scolded himself. *I can't go back now – I have to make it.* The dread of returning to the farm filled Will with a fresh surge of energy. He peddled as if his life depended on it. Which it sort of did, he supposed.

Some hours later, he arrived at the docks. He leapt off the bike and pushed it into a side street. His shaky legs barely held him up as he ran towards the harbour. He walked around the edge of the building, keeping to the shadows. Dozens of workers were scurrying back and forth. There were three ships in the dock; he had to make sure he got on the right one, and before sunrise. Elizabeth had told him she thought the name of the ship was Aristotle.

Will squinted at the sides of the ships. He was fairly sure it was the ship furthest away. *Oh no! I'm gonna have to make a run for it!*

He hid in the shadows for an unbearable length of time. Finally, the dockers stopped for a break. *It's now or never.* He lurched out of the darkness and darted across the yard to the ship, his heart thumping loudly. He sprinted up the gangway. *Made it!*

He searched urgently for somewhere to hide, eventually spotting a flight of steps leading below deck. They led onto a small platform where there was another flight down. Without glancing back, he carried on. He found himself in a short corridor with two doors leading off it. Opening the first door, he discovered a room full of machinery. The second room looked promising. It was stacked with boxes and barrels. *Perfect!* He squeezed into a small space behind one of the boxes.

Not long now! Home… I'm going home!

Before long the ship set sail, and the gentle swaying soothed Will to sleep.

– CHAPTER EIGHTEEN–

The Discovery

Will drifted through lurid dreams as the ship rocked and rolled.

What on earth was that? A tremendous bang jolted him awake. He could hear muffled shouting and banging above his head, but he couldn't make out what was being said. He groped in his pocket for his phone – at least it would help him to see.

Turning it on he realised the battery was close to running out; he switched it off again. He knew it wouldn't be much help in 1943, but he didn't want his last link with home snuffed out.

Sighing, he crept to the door and eased it open. The smell of burning was overpowering. Cupping his hand over his nose and mouth, he realised the ship must have been hit. He opened the door fully and stepped out into the corridor. Acrid smoke engulfed him instantly, making his eyes smart. He pulled his jumper over his mouth and tried to find the stairs. Adrenaline surged through his veins. His movements were clumsy as he felt along the bulkhead with his hands.

Surely the steps weren't that far when he came down? Stumbling along, he cracked his leg on something jutting out.

He reached out to steady himself and found the handrail for the stairs. *Thank God!* Gasping, he dragged himself up the ladders. He still couldn't see daylight. Why wasn't he at the top yet? Then he remembered: there were two sets of steps.

His breath rasped in his throat. It was becoming almost impossible to breathe. Shaking, he lunged forward, one arm outstretched in the hope that he would feel the edge of the step rail. Just as he thought his lungs would explode, his foot hit the stair. He clenched his teeth and made one last effort to climb the steps to freedom. He threw himself on the deck, his chest heaving.

'What have we here then?' a voice bellowed.

Will scrabbled to his feet. 'Sorry, sir—' His voice came out hoarse. 'I just… just… need to get to the city. Um, it's an emergency, you see. I thought you wouldn't mind if I just... sort of... had a lift?'

'A lift, eh? You mean stowaway, lad! Do you know what the offence is for stowaways?'

Will puffed up his chest and tried not to look scared. 'No, sir.'

'Prison! That's what it is!' He grabbed Will by the scruff of the neck.

'I'll deal with you later. Right now I have a ship to save, or none of us are going anywhere.' He shoved Will roughly out of the way. 'You'd better start bailing with the men.'

Will joined the long line of sailors passing water down to the hold, where the fire was raging.

'Faster! Faster!' roared the captain.

Will's arms ached with the effort, but at long last a holler came from below. 'She's out!'

Everyone cheered.

Will collapsed on the deck, wheezing. One of the sailors offered him a drink of water. He gulped it down, not sure it would be enough to quench his thirst.

'Right,' announced the captain. 'Time to deal with

you, lad.'

'Oh please, sir, just let me go,' Will said. 'My grandad's very ill. I must get to London.'

'London, is it?' said the captain, mocking him. 'Well then you're out of luck, lad. We're on a thirty-day supply run, not due to dock for a month. So there will be no lettin' you go. You're going to have to stay aboard and pull your weight.'

Will paled. 'Not going to dock?' he stammered. 'But I can't stay here.' His gaze took in the vast expanse of water; now was not the time to mention he couldn't swim!

He'd fallen into the neighbour's pond when he was five and had nearly drowned. It was only Rollo's frantic barking that had brought his mum running from the house. He was freezing when she'd dragged him out. After that he'd refused to ever go near water. No amount of persuading would make him have swimming lessons.

'Well it's that or chuck you overboard,' the captain said, losing patience.

Will realised he had no choice; he would have to find the courage to work on the ship and hope that he would get a safe passage home.

'Right, sir. I'll do my best.' Will tried saluting for good measure.

'Piper!' yelled the captain. 'Take this boy and find him a spare hammock, then set him to work in the galley.'

'Right-o, Captain! Come on, lad, let's go!'

Will cast an anxious look back at the sea. It was just thirty days, wasn't it?

Will finished throwing up and headed back to his hammock down below, clutching his now empty but still sore stomach. It didn't help that the hammock smelled of sweat, and the continuous noise of pipes clanging and banging as water rushed through them hurt Will's head.

'You'll be right as rain in a few days. The first week is the worst,' Piper said, his spotty face looming down from his hammock above Will.

It was stiflingly hot in the bunks. Will groaned, rubbing his tender stomach. 'I hope so,' he replied. He wished he'd tried to get to London some other way, but at least he had found a friend in Piper.

They worked together in the ship's kitchen. Piper had explained that this was called the galley. Will mostly had to peel vast amounts of potatoes and wash up. Piper told Will, rather grandly, that at seventeen he was training to be a chef.

'Why are you so desperate to get to London then?' Piper asked Will one day when they were mopping up.

Will stuck to his story. 'My grandad's ill. He doesn't have anyone to look after him. Don't you have family, Piper?'

Will still found it odd to address people by their surname, but the captain had informed him that's how it was done onboard ship. 'What's your surname, boy?' he had roared at Will the second day after his discovery. Will had cast his eyes around, not wanting to give his real name. 'Er, Crow, sir,' he'd said, his eyes alighting on a flight of birds. 'It's Will Crow.'

Piper stopped mopping to wipe his nose on his sleeve. 'Nah, not really. I have a sister. She brought me up, like, but she's married now with a nipper on the way.'

Will gave the floor a final flick with his mop. 'I don't think I could stand being at sea all the time. There's too much water for one thing,' he said with a shudder.

– CHAPTER NINETEEN–

All at Sea

After two weeks of continuous mopping, washing up and preparing food, Will felt ready to drop. He had muscles where once there had been only skin and bone. His back ached with trying to stand still as the ship rocked from side to side. But at least he had proved himself to the captain, and he was rewarded with some occasional time off.

As he sat on the deck and gazed out to sea, he wondered how his friends were doing. He had been doing a lot of thinking since being on the ship, and he had decided to write to Jim. Piper had told him they could send letters off once a month.

'Can I borrow some paper and a stamp?' Will asked Piper that night. They were sitting in the mess, a small room where they could relax if they weren't working or sleeping. Will squeezed in between a couple of the sailors who were reading.

'Sure, you writing home then?'

'Yes,' Will replied automatically. He found that lying came almost instinctively now. He sucked the end of the pen, thinking of Jim.

Dear Jim,

(Sorry I can't say Dad. It doesn't feel right.) I hope you are well. I am on board a ship and will be back in London very soon, I hope. I would like to come and see you and still hope you can help with my problem. Maybe you could come with me to see Mum?

Love, Will

The next morning the captain called them all up on deck. 'Change of plan, lads. We are weighing anchor tonight offshore. We need to pick up fuel. We will be staying around these waters for a few weeks now.'

Will put his hand up, forgetting he wasn't at school.

'Yes, Crow?'

'What coast are we near, sir?'

'You know better than to ask that, sonny. Careless

talk and all that. But I can tell you that we will be delayed considerably.' He gave a vicious grin.

Will felt bile rise in his throat. *Longer on this godforsaken ship, no thanks*, he thought.

'Piper, what country do you think that is?' Will asked after the meeting was over. He pointed at the shadowy land in the distance.

'Dunno, I have heard some of the lads say they think it's Kent. Why?'

'I need to get to it.' Will stomped his feet, trying to keep warm.

'Jump ship you mean?' Piper's eyes were as big as saucers.

'Yes, will you help me?'

Piper swallowed nervously.

'I can take a lifeboat and row under cover in the dark,' Will said. He puffed his chest out. 'I know I can make it.'

'You're mad,' Piper said, looking over the side. 'You'll drown.'

At the mention of water, Will's resolve wobbled, but then he thought of grandad sitting at home lonely and worried.

'I'm going anyway. I'll go tonight.'

Piper fiddled with his hat. He wanted to help Will but he didn't want to get into trouble. 'I'll help you lower the boat but then you're on your own.'

Stealthily Will and Piper made their way up to the deck. Will took in his surroundings. It all looked so different at night. The sea lapped at the boat, making the chains rattle against the sides. The ropes slithered around the gloomy deck like giant snakes. Will looked over at the black sea, his heart in his mouth. He didn't think he'd ever been so scared.

'Come on, help me to untie the knots,' Piper said in a whisper as he fumbled with the rope

Will's teeth began to chatter. 'I'm trying, but my fingers keep slipping.' His hands were numb with cold. He tugged harder on the rope, finally freeing the boat. Eventually they lowered it into the water with a gentle splash. Piper threw the ladder over the side for Will.

'Hurry, Will, before the Captain does his rounds.'

Will flung his arms around Piper in a hasty hug before lowering himself over the side, his feelings in turmoil.

'I can do this. I can do this,' he repeated to himself over and over. He slowly placed his feet on the ladder rungs, counting each step until he felt the rocking of the boat beneath him. Cautiously he sat down and took up the oars. 'Thanks, Piper,' he said as he slowly started to row away.

Will rowed and rowed, only concentrating on the tiny speck of light he could see in the distance. His arms ached, and his back twitched every time he pulled on the oars. Licking his lips, he could taste salty water as the sea spray hit his face and blurred his eyes, but he dared not let go of the oars for a second.

Gradually the land inched ever closer until he came to a little cove, where he beached the boat. Exhausted he pulled in the oars. *I've made it!* he thought elatedly before sleep overtook him.

A seagull crowed loudly nearby, waking him with a jerk. He fumbled for his glasses; they had slipped off his nose as he slept. The sun was just rising above the horizon. Gingerly he stepped off the boat. His teeth chattered as a cool wind blew across the headland. Freezing, Will stood up and did star jumps to warm his body up. *Now what?* He thought. He would have to walk to the nearest town or village and find out exactly where he was. He shuddered, hoping Piper hadn't got it wrong and he was in Scotland or worse. Hitching his backpack over his shoulder, he started the long climb up the bank to the top.

Breathing hard he looked around; there was a rough path leading away from the coast, and he could see a church spire in the distance. He started to walk towards it. He wondered if the captain had noticed his absence yet, or if Piper would get into trouble – he hoped not. His stomach growled; he hadn't eaten for hours. He fished out a sea biscuit from his pocket and nibbled on it slowly as he walked.

Arriving in the small village, Will could see a street market was taking place. At least now he would find out where he was.

He stopped at the first stall. 'Excuse me?'

'Yes?' A plump woman, selling fish and wearing her hair in curlers tied with a scarf, replied.

'What town is this?'

135

'You lost your memory or something?' She re-arranged the fish, their glassy eyes staring accusingly at Will.

'No, I'm an orphan. Our house was bombed. I walked through the night.' Will had been working on his lie all morning.

'Oh, sorry to hear that, love.' She gazed at him sympathetically. 'You should go and see Betty.' She pointed at a woman several stalls away. 'She'll find you somewhere to stay.'

'Thanks.' Will turned to leave.

'Oh, and this is Faversham, love,' she shouted after him.

'Thanks,' Will called back, walking quickly away. He didn't want to ask her where Faversham was in case she got suspicious. He'd ask someone else. He spotted a lady selling tea from a giant earn. Piper had given him some money before they parted company. 'Here,' he'd said, handing Will a hanky heavy with coins, its corners tied in a knot to stop them spilling out. 'For your travels.'

Will drank the tea gratefully. 'How far is it to London?' he asked as he handed her the mug back.

'London?' she screwed up her eyes. 'I don't rightly know, couple of hours on the bus at least, I'd guess. Never been myself.' She cackled. 'You going to seek your fortune?'

Will grinned in reply, before going to sit on a nearby bench. So he knew he wasn't far from London; all he had to do was find out about the busses and, hey presto, he'd be back before he could blink. Cheerfully he swung his legs. At last things seemed to be going his way.

– CHAPTER TWENTY–

Getting Closer

Will's stomach growled, reminding him that he was hungry. He decided to explore the village shop before catching the bus. He wasn't sure what he could buy for a few pennies, but there had to be something. The bell above the door tinkled cheerfully as he pushed it open.

An elderly man wearing a white coat and a flat cap came out from behind a long counter that ran the length of the shop. 'Hello, lad, and what can I get for you?'

Will looked at the shelves lining the rest of the shop walls. There was very little choice: no crisps, no sweets, no sandwiches. It was nothing like the shop near his house, which sold everything you could think of. Then he spotted some biscuits.

'Can I have a packet of those, please?' he said, pointing. He hoped he'd have enough money.

'Got your book?'

'Book?' Will looked blankly at the man.

'Ration book?' he snapped, holding his hand out.

Will recalled Frank and Charlie telling him about rationing in London, but it hadn't seemed so bad when they were in the country. All he wanted was one lousy packet of biscuits. He'd had enough of wartime Britain.

Blushing, he said, 'Sorry, sir. I forgot to bring it.'

'No coupon, no biscuits. Sorry, son.' The man turned and placed the pack back on the shelf.

'I can pay for them,' Will said, holding out the coins in his palm.

The grocer pursed his lips. 'I need to stamp your book. You know the rules. Come back with it and you can buy the biscuits.'

Will banged the door as he left. 'Stupid, stupid war,' he muttered to himself as he walked up the road, his stomach rumbling.

He'd just have to wait until he saw Jim. Remembering he had a bus to catch, he stopped a passer-by. 'Can you tell me where I get the bus to London from, please? And what time does it leave?'

'You've missed today's bus, lad. It leaves from the church at 10am sharp.'

'Isn't there another?' Will asked.

'Yes, lad, tomorrow.' The man looked at Will as if he was stupid.

Will kicked a stone viciously. *Why does everything have to be so difficult?* he thought. *How can there only be one bus a day?* He sighed, wishing he could click his heels and be back home like Dorothy in *The Wizard of Oz*.

Instead he was stuck in Faversham for another night with nowhere to stay. He walked back through the village and out towards the countryside, looking back from time to time to make sure he could always see the church spire. He knew that the Home Guard had been ordered to remove all signposts, and he didn't want to get lost. He never thought that watching *Dad's Army* with his grandad would offer such practical knowledge.

In the distance he saw a cluster of apple trees behind a low wall. Will hopped over and helped himself to a couple of juicy apples. Sinking his teeth into the cool flesh, he walked on, looking for somewhere to sleep for the night.

He passed several fields before coming across a derelict barn. Checking no one was around, he ducked inside. *This should be okay*, he thought. *At least it has a roof.* He dragged a straw bale towards the entrance and sat down. He tried not to think about the spiders and rats that might be lurking in the dark corners. Instead he thought about what he would say to Jim when he saw him next. He really wanted to find out why Jim had left him and his mum, but he wasn't sure if he'd have the courage to ask him. He closed his eyes and let his mind drift.

Will yawned and stretched. He must have dropped off at some point. He did remember that some bats had flown out of the barn as he was trying to get to sleep.

Cold and stiff he walked slowly back to the village. He wanted to be in plenty of time for the bus. But he did find time to stop and help himself to another couple of apples as he passed by the orchard.

A few people had already gathered by the church. Joining them, he lent against the wall, listening to their conversations.

They chattered on, discussing the raids and how London had been bombed every night recently. He still couldn't believe how accepting people were of the situation. Will's stomach churned. He hoped Jim was all right. He crossed his fingers behind his back, wishing for good luck.

'I hope it's coming today,' said one of the women looking at her watch.

'I did hear on the wireless that some of the roads were impassable,' said another. 'I don't know which ones though.'

'Hopefully not the ones we want,' another joked. She peered up the road hoping to see the bus coming around the corner.

'Is it usually on time?' Will asked, biting his cheek.

'Yes, duck, he always tries to be, but there's no accounting for the bombs and the state of the roads.' She looked at her watch again.

'What time is it now?' asked Will.

'Five and twenty-past.'

They hung around until eleven.

'That's it, I'm not waiting any longer. It's obviously

not coming today,' a woman said as she made to leave. 'No point in you standing there, lad.'

'But I have to get to London today.' Will's voice shook. He couldn't stay another night. He just couldn't. Close to tears, he said, 'Is there any other way I can get to London? I have to see my grandad.'

'Can't it wait until tomorrow?'

'No!' snapped Will.

'You could try the train,' said another woman.

'Train?' repeated Will.

'Yes, duck, the train. Course, I don't know if you'd get on. It's mostly full of troops.'

'I can try,' Will said. 'Can you direct me to the station, please?'

'Go out of the village, past the pig farm and it's about a mile or so from there.'

'Thanks.'

Will lost no time in heading out of the village, repeating with every step, 'I'm going to get the train. I'm going to get the train.'

When he arrived at the station, a kindly faced man

beamed at him from behind the ticket counter.

'Where to, son?'

'London please.'

'Single or return?'

'Single please.'

'That will cost a joey, lad, platform two.'

Will fumbled through the coins in his hand, not really sure what he was looking for.

'That one.' The clerk pointed at a twelve-sided brass coin. Will handed it to him and received a green ticket in return.

'Thanks.' Will shoved it into his pocket and raced onto the platform, worried the train would leave without him.

The guard paced up and down the platform, impatiently slamming doors as people jumped on. Will let out a sigh of relief as he heard the carriage door clunk shut behind him. The train was full of army, navy and airforce personnel. There was standing room only, but Will didn't care. They were in high spirits, joking and singing patriotic songs as the train sped towards London. Will found himself tapping his foot and humming along. The atmosphere couldn't have been more different from his last trip. Finally he really was on his way.

– CHAPTER TWENTY-ONE–

Back in London

The train puffed along at a steady pace, stopping at various stations en route. Gradually the leafy countryside gave way to houses and factories; drab, bombed and covered in soot, they looked like relics of a ghost town.

Finally, they arrived at the station. Will walked out onto the street. The heavy air caught the back of his throat. Within minutes his eyes began to sting. *I haven't missed this,* he thought. He headed for King George Road. *I can find my way to Jim's house from there.*

He walked slowly, picking his way through the rubble-strewn streets. London had obviously taken a hammering since he was last there. Wherever there was a spare bit of wall or doorway, there were posters. 'Careless Talk Costs Lives' and 'Dig for Victory' were two slogans he recognised from the schoolroom in

Shirehampton.

His memory flipped back. How he missed Frank and Charlie. He wished he could tell them he was back in London. He was reminded of Dr Carrot and Potato Pete, characters made up by the government to encourage people to eat healthily. Charlie had thought it hilarious and would sometimes pretend to be Dr Carrot when they were eating their lunches.

Will's chest constricted. He needed to focus.

Eventually he was at the end of King George Road. He walked down the length of the street, back to where they had tried to get through. His palms sweaty, he wondered if it would still be barricaded. He slowed his pace as he came to the spot where he had been trapped. It had been tidied up. The bricks had been stacked and the wood lay neatly in a pile. He wondered if Jim knew. He couldn't wait to tell him. With renewed effort he hurried on.

His heart raced as he lifted his hand to knock on the door. *What if Jim wasn't home, or worse, what if he didn't want to see him?* He ran a hand through his tousled hair.

'Will!' Jim cried, opening the door.

'Yes, it's me.' Will's voice cracked.

'Come in, come in.' Jim pulled Will into a hug before shutting the door behind him. 'Let's go through to the back room. I expect you'd like a cup of tea?'

'I'd love a cup of tea,' Will said, flopping into a comfy chair.

Jim cut two large doorstops of fresh white bread and slathered them in butter. 'Here you go, lad. You look half-starved,' he said, putting the plate in front of Will.

Will tucked in; never had bread and butter tasted so delicious. Back home he would have laughed if his mum had told him he could only have bread and butter.

Jim placed two cups of tea on the table and sat down opposite Will.

'Where have you been?' he asked. 'Last I heard, Auntie Doris had sent you back to your sister? I assumed that you had found a way back home.'

'Didn't you get my letter?' Will said between mouthfuls of bread.

Jim stroked his beard. 'Letter? No, I never had a letter.'

'I wrote to you from the ship I was on.'

'Ship?' Jim's jaw dropped. 'I think you'd better start

at the beginning, lad.'

Will told him about how Frank and Charlie had persuaded him to go with them and how he'd ended up on a farm near Bristol.

'It was horrid there,' he said with a shudder. 'The farmer was crazy. Frank said he thought he was a spiv.'

Jim nodded knowingly. 'There's plenty about. Just as well you didn't get tangled up with him.' He sipped his tea. 'How are the twins getting along?' he asked.

'They love it there. I tried to get them to come back with me but they didn't want to.'

'And how did you get back then?'

'Well…' Will told him about the ship and how he'd been worried that he'd end up in France or somewhere. 'Piper helped me to escape,' he said.

'You took a massive risk, lad.' Jim's eyes narrowed. 'Wartime is not a game. You could have easily been killed.'

Will scowled. 'Maybe, but I couldn't stay there, could I? My place is in the future. I have to get back to the time rift.' He banged his fist on the table.

'Steady on, son. Look I'll make us another cuppa and we talk some more.'

Will felt his heart leap as he watched him move around the kitchen. *He called me son*, he thought. Yawning, he realised just how tired of adventuring he was. He wanted his mum, Rollo and grandad.

'Have you been back to the site?' Jim asked.

'Yes, I walked that way from the station.'

Jim cut up some homemade fruitcake and placed it on the table.

'Do you think you can get me through?' Will said, chomping on a slice. It was very chewy, with a bit of a funny taste. Nothing like his mum's cake.

Jim's gripped his cup his knuckles white. 'Probably,' he said quietly.

Will studied him for a while. 'If you're really my dad why did you leave us?' he said abruptly.

Jim let out a long breath. 'I was young then,' he said.

'So you just abandoned my mum and forgot all about us!' Will leapt up his eyes blazing.

'I didn't know about you,' he said gently. 'Sit down.' He gestured towards the chair. 'And I'll tell you what happened.'

Will hesitated. He was angry with Jim, he was angry

about being stuck here, and he was angry with himself for caring. He jutted out his chin.

'Fine,' he said, sitting on the edge of the seat. 'I'll listen but then I want you to take me back.'

Jim nodded. 'OK, son.' He cleared his throat before beginning. 'As you know I found the time rift and travelled to the future. It was a bit of fun to go to the future from time to time, but then I met Susan, your mum.' He took a sip of tea. 'We just clicked. I went to see her more and more but...' He hesitated. 'It became clear that she wasn't living her life. It was like she was on hold, just waiting for my visits. Do you understand?' Will nodded, his hands twisting in his lap.

'It was the same for me,' Jim said. 'I couldn't settle properly. I was always thinking about going to see Susan.'

'Why didn't you just stay?' Will interrupted.

Jim put his hands over Will's. 'Would you stay here, now, with me?' he asked. 'Of course you might think you could, but in time you would resent it. You'd miss your mum, your friends and the comforts of your home. I wanted to stay, but we decided that it would be impossible. On my last trip I told Susan that I wouldn't be coming back, that I had to let her go. She agreed it was for the best, but begged me to come back one last time. A proper goodbye, she said. I agreed to come back the following week. We kissed and I left. That was the last time I ever saw her.' His eyes glistened with unshed tears.

'But why?' Will jumped up again, his head throbbing from trying to take it all in. 'Why didn't you go back?'

'Because, son, that's when the shop was sold, and I couldn't find a way.' He sighed deeply. 'It wasn't to be.' His shoulders slumped. 'I think she thought she was pregnant with you, and that's why she wanted me to go and see her again. She would have been sure by then. Maybe she thought we could work it out.' He gazed into Will's eyes, a mirror of his own. 'I never married, you know. I still miss her.'

Will sat very still. *Was this his dad?* If only he could be sure. Then he remembered the video clip on his phone; he could show it to Jim, ask him if the photo was him. Hopefully he'd have enough battery left.

He took his phone from his pocket and switched it on. He loaded the video. 'I took this the day I left,' he said. 'Is this photo of you?' He played the clip.

Jim gasped. 'That's her.' He pointed at the screen. Will's mum smiled out. Will had forgotten he'd filmed her in the kitchen.

'And the photo?'

Jim watched on. He leaned in closer as the film showed the small photo frame. 'Yes, that's me,' he said, his voice barely a whisper.

Will snapped the phone off. 'How could you!' His voice quivered. 'Because of you I've never fitted in. I've never made friends easily.' He paced around the kitchen. 'You've hurt me and you've hurt my mum!' He burst into noisy tears.

Jim stared at the floor. 'I did try and come back,' he said. 'It just wasn't possible after the grocers shut. I've thought about your mum every day since!'

Will bit his lip, his thoughts spinning. He wanted to believe Jim. But… He fidgeted in the chair.

'Why didn't you try harder. I don't know, break into the shop or something?'

'I tried, son, I really did.' He let out a long, lone sigh.

Will pulled his knees up to his chest and circled his arms around them. 'I wish you had come back,' he said, his voice a whisper.

Jim put his arm around Will.

'I know, son, and I'm sorry. For what it's worth, so do I.'

Will looked across at Jim. He was sat in front of his dad; that was all he'd ever wanted. He flung himself into Jim's arms. 'I'm sorry, I…' His voice choked.

Jim hugged him tightly. 'I'm sorry too, son. Why don't you stay with me tonight, and I'll take you back tomorrow after I've fed you up a bit. We don't want your mother thinking I can't look after you.'

Will gave him a watery smile.

After tea Jim switched on the wireless. The speaker crackled and hissed as he tuned into the BBC. Will listened silently. It was very different from his iPod or even the radio his mum kept on the kitchen windowsill.

'I've been thinking,' he said. 'Why don't we record a message for Mum on my phone?'

'Er…' Jim lent forward in his chair.

'It would be great.' Will switched his phone on and pressed record. 'I'm sure she'd love to hear from you.'

He pointed it at Jim. 'Say something.'

'Um…' Jim stroked his beard. 'Hello, Sue, how are you?' he paused. 'I'm truly sorry I never came back, but I couldn't,' his voice cracked. 'I've thought about you a lot. You were the only girl for me.'

Just then Will's phone started to beep, shutting down as it went flat.

– CHAPTER TWENTY-TWO –

The Reunion

After a full night's sleep, Will was grateful for the steaming bowl of porridge that Jim put down in front of him.

'Eat up then, son,' he said, smiling at Will.

Will ate his porridge while his dad combed his beard. 'Why did you grow a beard, Dad?' he asked.

'Just one of those things. I got fed up of shaving all the time, and it just sort of grew and grew. Don't think I'd like to be without it now.' He put the brush down. 'We should leave shortly,' he said as he looked out of the window at the grey skies above.

'I'm ready,' Will said, shovelling the last of his porridge down.

Jim unhooked a knapsack from behind the door and checked its contents before hitching it over his shoulder. 'Just a few things we might need,' he said.

They strolled down the road together. Will thought about Frank and Charlie. 'Will you tell the twins that I came back?'

'Of course I will. I'm sure they'll want to hear that you're home safe.'

'I wish I could write to them.' Will thrust his hands into his pockets, drawing his shoulders up.

Jim patted his arm. 'That's one of the difficulties of time travel. Making friends and then not being able to stay in touch.' He hesitated. 'And wondering what happened to them.'

Will frowned. He knew what Jim was referring to. His fingers curled around the tin soldier nestled in his pocket.

'I want you to have this,' he said, pulling it free and passing it to Jim.

'A tin soldier! I used to play with these when I was a lad.'

'I found it in Grandad's air raid shelter. I think it's a lucky soldier.'

'I'll take great care of him.' Jim slid the soldier into his jacket pocket.

'Then you'll have something to remember me by,' Will said softly.

'I will,' Jim said, his chin trembling.

They walked on in silence until they came to the bombed out shop.

'Here we are then.' Jim said, his jaw clenching as he glanced at Will.

'What do we do now?' Will bounced from foot to foot, barely able to conceal his excitement.

'We see if we can get in.' Jim observed the empty street. 'Follow me.' He climbed over the pile of bricks, walked around the corner and across to the derelict storeroom minus its door. He breathed a sigh of relief. Fishing his torch from his bag, he carefully made his way inside. Will followed, his breath echoing in the small room. Jim shone the torch over the bricks on the back wall. 'There it is,' he said.

'What?' Will asked.

He shone the torch at one of the bricks. 'That one's loose. When you pull it out the time rift opens. At least I hope it will,' he muttered. He turned to look at Will. 'I guess this is it then.' He pulled him into a tight hug.

'Wait!' Will pulled free. 'Why don't you come with me?'

'Come with you?' Jim sounded startled.

'Yes!' Excited by his idea, Will's eyes sparkled. 'You could come and meet Mum, explain to her. Please, Dad?'

Jim raised his eyebrows. 'I don't know, son. Look how risky it's been. We don't even know if it will work yet.'

'But if it does, then you know you can get back. Come on, Dad. Let's do it together.' He took Jim's hand in his. 'We'll do it together. Ready?'

Jim studied Will's face. He looked tired and older somehow. He couldn't let him down again. But he couldn't risk getting stuck in the future. He shuffled his feet and cleared his throat. 'Son—' he started.

'Dad… please,' Will repeated.

Jim opened his mouth to argue, then stopped. He tilted his head from side to side, giving himself time to think. What choice did he have? He'd just have to hope he could get back. He squeezed Will's fingers. 'Come on then.' He reached up and pulled the brick free.

There was a sudden whoosh of cold air. Will could see a door faintly in the distance. *This is it.* He walked forward a few steps and pushed hard.

He fell into the air raid shelter. Wiping the dust from his glasses, he realised he was alone. 'That can't be right,' he muttered, and without thinking he turned and walked back through the door.

'Dad? Why did you let go?'

'I didn't, son.' He ran a hand through his beard. 'Maybe I can't get through?'

'Don't be silly, of course you can. Come on, let's try again. We'll run this time.' He took hold of Jim's hand. 'After three,' he said. 'One, two, three, now!' They ran to the doorway. Once again Will fell through onto the shelter floor alone. He scratched his head in puzzlement. Standing, he went back again.

'I can't come through, son.' Jim's voice broke. 'You have to go back by yourself.'

'No!' Will stamped his foot, 'You must be able to somehow.'

Tears ran down Jim's face. 'I wish I could.'

Will looked at him in horror. 'But I can't leave you now.' His voice rose in anguish. 'Please try again?'

'There's no point, son, we've tried.' He pulled a

handkerchief from his pocket and wiped his eyes.

Will gulped, tears trickling down his nose. 'But you're my dad.' He sobbed.

'I know and I always will be.' Jim held on to him tightly. Clearing his throat, he said, 'Come on, it's time for you to go. We can't risk the rift not working.' He turned Will to face the rift. 'Goodbye, son, God speed.' He quickly pushed Will forward before he had a chance to change his mind.

Will lay on the shelter floor. 'Goodbye, Dad,' he said. Exhausted, he must have slept for a few minutes. His eyes opened slowly. He thought he could hear barking. He shook his head. *No, that wasn't right, there weren't any dogs here.* He sat up. There it was again: a definite barking.

'Rollo!' he cried. 'Rollo, I'm back!' Scrambling to his feet, he rushed out of the shelter into the glorious sunshine of Grandad's garden. Rollo bounded over, nearly knocking Will off his feet. 'Oh, Rollo, I've missed you so much.' Will wrapped his arms around Rollo's furry neck.

'Woof woof,' replied Rollo, licking Will enthusiastically.

'Where have you been hiding?' a voice said from behind him suddenly.

Will looked up startled. 'Grandad,' he shrieked, running over the grass to meet him.

'Steady on, you'll have me over in a minute.' Grandad ruffled his hair.

'Will, you're absolutely filthy!' his mum said, coming out of the house. 'What on earth have you been doing?'

'I've been trapped in World War Two,' Will said.

She laughed, 'Honestly, Will, that imagination of yours will get you into trouble one of these days.'

'But I have,' he said with a scowl.

'Now, now,' Grandad said. 'Let's not fall out, hmm? I'll get you a drink then you can tell us what you've been up to.'

Will gulped the lemonade down, coughing and spluttering. His eyes watered. 'I thought it was water,' he said. 'I forgot we had lemonade in the future.'

His mum and grandad shared a knowing look. 'Will, you didn't go to the past, stop pretending now,' his mum said.

'But I did! I met Dad and everything.'

His mum turned away.

'Now don't go upsetting your mum, Will,' Grandad said.

Will puffed out his cheeks. 'There's an air raid shelter at the bottom of your garden, that's how I got through.'

'I'd forgotten all about that,' Grandad said. 'Is that where you have been playing?'

Will rolled his eyes. Clearly they weren't going to believe him. He gave up. He didn't know whether to feel pleased or cross.

That night, back in his own room, having charged his phone, he played back the video of his dad. He should go and show his mum, and then she'd have to believe him. He nudged Rollo off the bed.

'Mum,' he called. 'I've got something to show you.'

'Just a minute. I'm just taking a cake out of the oven.'

Will walked downstairs. She was singing along to the radio and dancing round the kitchen. He recalled listening to the radio with his dad; suddenly it seemed so long ago.

Will looked at her, and then at the phone in his hand.

She was so happy he just couldn't do it.

And he pressed delete.

Also available from Candy Jar Books

The Norris Girls by Nigel Hinton

Dad is away in a dangerous place, but life must go on for the Norris girls.

Beth dreams of being in the school musical, especially when super cool Josh gets the lead part.

Georgy trains every day, trying to win a place in the Inter-Counties Athletics Championships but first she has to beat her arch-rival, Layla.

And Katie wants an animal to look after – a dog or a cat or a rabbit would do, but if she could choose one thing in the whole world it would be a pony.

Filled with tears and laughter, heartache and longing, this is Little Women for the twenty-first century.

Keeping Clear of Paradise Street
by Brian Moses

In the 1950s there was no Internet, no iPhones, no games consoles, no colour TV. Sounds grim?

Actually there was good stuff too. What kind of stuff? Well how about... secret tunnels... flea circuses... Saturday morning cinema...
cows in the back garden?

Cows in the back garden!? Yep. The past was a strange place.

And Brian Moses was there. Of course, he wasn't so 'old' back then. He was around your age. Old enough to be your friend! Read stories of killer crabs, teachers armed with baseball bats, and grenades that washed up on the beach.